CLANCY MARTIN

LOVE IN CENTRAL AMERICA

Complete and Unabridged

ULVERSCROFT
Leicester

First published in Great Britain in 2016 by
Harvill Secker
an imprint of Vintage
London

First Large Print Edition
published 2017
by arrangement with
Vintage
Penguin Random House
London

A catalogue record for this book is available
from the British Library.

ISBN 978–1–4448–3372–0

Published by
F. A. Thorpe (Publishing)
Anstey, Leicestershire
Set by Words & Graphics Ltd.
Anstey, Leicestershire
Printed and bound in Great Britain by
T. J. International Ltd., Padstow, Cornwall

This book is printed on acid-free paper

LOVE IN CENTRAL AMERICA

Cheating on your husband is like doing cocaine. It's rarely pleasurable, but try quitting . . . Brett is in Mexico, away from her husband Paul, when she meets up with his captivating banker Eduard. Whilst Paul has always been a stabilising influence, Eduard encourages her dark side, and her sobriety is soon slipping from her grasp. Finding herself on a downward spiral of sneaking off with her new lover and blacking out in hotels, Brett still has sufficient clarity to see that she is sabotaging her life — but is unable to stop . . .

For ZC

Thank you for never giving up

'This wasn't invented, it really happened'
— Alejandro Zambra

1

One of us had to watch our hotel in Tulum during the storm, so I was flying into Cancun International then renting a car. The hurricane had closed all of the airports on the coast, and my flight was delayed, and then cancelled. As I was walking out of the airport, I heard an announcement my flight was boarding. It was the last flight into Cancun. When I got to the hotel, I told the story to the clerk and she laughed and upgraded me to a suite. 'It will just sit empty anyway,' she told me, as though she were apologizing for the change. 'We're getting flooded with cancellations.' I asked her for an envelope, put sixty dollars into it, and handed it back to her. The room was enormous, with a dining room table, a kitchen in case you'd brought your own cook, and floor-to-ceiling windows with long views of the ocean. The waves were huge and confused in the storm, and they stretched as far as I could see in the rain.

It was ten in the morning.

2

I paced around the room, looked at myself in the mirror, went to the bathroom, and then opened my computer on the desk. I sat for a few minutes, trying to tell myself I could write, and then moved to the bed and read the room service menu. When I came to the wine list in the back, I closed it. I went over to the window, leaned my forehead against the cold glass, and stared down the ten stories. My forehead made a smear on the glass. I got a Coke Light from the minibar. Then I took off my shoes and jacket and sat on the couch to call Paul.

'I'm already lonely for you,' I said. It was the day after Christmas, and the truth was I was glad for a break. Paul's boys had been out of school for a week and his family had visited for the holidays. His mother was a friend of mine but she had a way of taking over the house. She was a devoted grand-mother but the boys were nervous around her, because she was wealthy and uptight and dressed carefully each morning. Paul's father was there now — his parents were divorced — and he was clingy and demanding. He

2

frequently needed to go to the pharmacy or the grocery store to buy things. But he hated Mexico City — they were from a small town in Massachusetts — and he'd get lost if he drove himself. He was good with the boys but he liked to tell us how to parent them. Also, after a few days Paul felt like he had a third child in the house.

'My dad is driving me crazy. He keeps getting angry when I won't stay up and watch a movie with him. We watched two Burt Reynolds movies last night and he wasn't satisfied. Hurry home,' he said. 'I need you here right now.'

'I'm sorry. One of us had to go. It's three nights. I really ought to be here for at least a week. And I've already got a little writing done. It's so quiet here, with the hurricane, there's nothing else to do. I'll drive down to Tulum tomorrow or the next day.'

'Don't get on the road until the weather is better. You're writing? That's good. I told you. How's the Ritz?'

'It hasn't changed. Anyway, without you, it's a room. It doesn't matter.'

We didn't have anything to talk about but I didn't want him to get off the phone.

3

I called my friend Sadie, a doctor from Galveston, Texas. I hadn't seen her in a couple of years, and she was driving to Cancun to meet me for the weekend. She wasn't afraid of the storm.

I hadn't told Paul that Sadie was coming. Not for any reason. I knew it would annoy him. It was understood that this was a necessary but unfortunate work trip that one of us had to make and since they were his boys I was the one going, and I wasn't supposed to enjoy myself. But I should have told him I'd invited Sadie down. He had never been crazy about Sadie. 'She's trouble,' he always said about her. 'All psychiatrists are crazy, But she's not just ordinary crazy. She's crazy about sex. She tries to sleep with me every time she visits.'

'Paul, she does not.' Maybe she did, a little. But she didn't mean anything by it.

★   ★   ★

'Man! These roads are for shit. I'd turn around right now if it weren't for you.'

4

'I'm glad you're coming. Thanks. You want to go to Pobrecito's? I'll make a reservation.'

'You're buying. Hell, I'm almost in town, I'll come to your hotel. No, you're not invited, buddy, sorry. I'm dropping you off the minute we cross the border, like you said. Del la What? That on the coast?'

'What?' I had no idea what she was talking about. 'That's where they catch those green lobsters, right?'

'Tell me you didn't pick up a hitchhiker, Sadie.'

'I have you on the speakerphone, Brett, watch what you say.' I heard her pick up the phone. 'He's a college kid. No? Well, what's with the bandana? You want any of this? Okay, fine. Well, just hold it, would ya? It's a pipe, buddy, it don't bite.'

'Sadie, I gotta go.'

'Can you believe this rain? Beautiful, actually. All the colors.'

'Sadie, you're stoned. I'll see you when you get here. Just valet under my name.'

'You just called. Alright, fine. Set up that restaurant.'

I thought about calling Paul back but I knew he was busy with his dad and the boys. I needed to work. Before I started, I checked my email. Three emails from an Italian publisher panicking about a manuscript I had promised him for months. Dozens of emails from *Fab, Dwell,* and *Tablet*. A request to blurb a book. Fan mail. An invitation to sit on someone's doctoral dissertation. I started to switch into Word when I saw there was one from Paul's banker. 'I'm in Cancun,' was the header. 'Do you have time for a cup of coffee today or tonight? Paul said you're here. I was supposed to be in Panama, but I'm stuck with everybody else. They say I'll get a flight tomorrow. Yrs, Eduard.'

Eduard and I had met briefly once at a party nearly a decade before, but I didn't remember it. I only knew because Paul told me so.

'He's not the kind of man you would notice,' Paul said. 'He's old, a bit chubby, and he doesn't know how to dress.'

I didn't want to meet with Eduard but thought I probably should.

Plus, now if I met Eduard, Paul would find out Sadie was in Cancun.

★ ★ ★

I wrote to Eduard. 'I have a friend in town from Texas, a psychiatrist I've known since high school, but if you want to meet us, it would be great. I'd love to hang out. What's a good bar? You'd be doing me a favor, in fact.

6

My friend Sadie is a drinker, and this way she'll have a drinking buddy.'

Eduard wrote back immediately: 'I don't know the bars in Cancun. I'll try to find a place close to your hotel. Paul said you're at the Ritz-Carlton?'

4

Sadie came up to my room around six.

'Wow, look at this place. I should have just stayed with you.'

'That's what I said. You can. Cancel your room.'

'No, you know me. I sometimes stay up late.' She laughed. I could see she was still stoned. 'I'm going to make a drink. You want a club soda?'

I told her the news.

'Man, I thought it was going to be girls' night out,' she said. 'What about that horse place we were planning on? I want to see those horses. Cowboys! Mexican cowboys are still the real thing. I thought we had reservations.'

'Oh, I changed it to tomorrow. This won't take long. We'll have one drink with him, then we can hit the town. Wherever you want to go.'

'Boring. You've been doing this to me for twenty-five years. Always some man.'

'I've been doing it to you? Please. He's not a man, Sadie. He's Paul's banker.'

Sadie rolled her eyes.

'Those days are behind me. We're old women. We're practically middle-aged.'

'Speak for yourself,' Sadie said. She was two years younger than me.

5

Eduard had picked an expensive bar in a basement in the old town. It took the taxi almost an hour to find the place. It was packed. The ceilings were low and the zinc bar stretched the entire length of the room. It was lit with dozens of bare Edison bulbs, and on the back wall they had glass cabinets filled with taxidermy molds and instruments. They'd have to redo the whole place in two years, I thought. New Mexico in old Cancun.

'This place is cool,' Sadie said. 'This is like a bar in New York. You wouldn't even know where you were if it weren't for all the Mexicans.'

Sadie had red hair. She had freckles on the bridge of her nose, and was slender with extraordinary legs and excellent posture. She was pretty in a way that made women hate and worship her.

I ordered her a martini and watched the door for Eduard. I was worried I wouldn't recognize him — I had no picture in my mind at all — and so I stared at all the men who came and went. An hour passed. Sadie told me a long story about one of her patients who was emotionally abusive to her husband. After three years of treatment, the woman broke down and confessed that she was not married.

'Now that's a woman who's fucking crazy,' she said. 'No better word for her. What the hell am I supposed to do with this woman? She still comes to see me. There's a novel in that one for you. You can use it to break your slump.'

I said, 'Maybe you should write it.'

I wondered if I could have gotten the night wrong. I checked my email on my phone.

'Where the hell is he? I thought a banker worked for you, not the other way around. I'm hungry. What time did he say?'

'Nine.'

'Shit, it's quarter after ten, and we haven't had any dinner. I'm starving. I'm getting a hamburger. Do you want a burger? Rare?'

Sadie got a hamburger, and her third double martini. I ordered things I thought Eduard might like, things that wouldn't go cold: olives, cheese, salami, roasted peppers, anchovies, lobster. The bartender recommended the truffle fries so I got those too.

'And one more Coke Light, if you don't mind. Sorry. I drink these things like water.'

'You know those are bad for you,' the bartender said. He smiled. 'Poison. Let me

11

make you a ginger ale. Trust me. Do you like eucalyptus?'

I shrugged, and he turned to start on my drink.

6

'Man that bartender is hot,' Sadie said. It was noisy but she said it loud enough for him to hear. 'He totally hit on you. Did you see that?' She raised her voice. 'It's funny because I'm the one who's interested. In him.' The bartender turned and looked at her. 'You,' she said, and raised her drink.

Sadie's husband was wealthy. He was handsome and young, but she had never been in love with him. She was happy in her marriage, but slept with other men. 'Hell, he knows,' she always said. 'But he doesn't know what he doesn't want to know, and I can keep my mouth shut.'

Paul had asked me to make a similar promise when we first started dating. 'Life is long, and you may cheat on me one day,' he said. 'If you do, just promise me you won't tell me about it.'

'I'll never cheat on you,' I said, but still I promised. I never had. 'This is a great burger,' Sadie said. 'You should have a burger. I'm gonna have another one. They're so tiny it's like a slider. In Galveston they'd serve you three of these.'

'I guess I'll get one too,' I said.

They had a clothing rack at the bottom of the stairs and a man was taking off a white windbreaker. He hung it on a hanger. He was wearing weird black leather gloves, and he took time getting them off his hands and into his coat pockets. That can't be him, I thought. He was dressed stylishly. He wore a black suit. The pants were tailored tight to his legs. He had a grey shirt on and a narrow grey tie. Contrary to what Paul said, he had hair. It was cut short, but growing long. He smiled and waved.

'Man, is that him?' Sadie said. 'Tell me that's him. That's not a banker. That's a fuckmaster prince.'

'I don't know what you are talking about.' I stood to meet him.

'Seriously,' Sadie was saying. 'He looks like Benicio Del Toro.'

Eduard walked up quickly and I held out my hand. He pushed it aside, hugged me, and gave me a kiss on the cheek. His lips were cold from outside. He took a seat at the bar.

'You know what? You look like a movie star,' Sadie said. 'Brett said you were like an ordinary man. I mean — you don't look like a banker.'

'Brett said I was ordinary?'

He winked at me and ordered a whiskey.

14

'Make it a double,' I said to the bartender, leaning forward so Sadie and Eduard wouldn't hear. 'And water down her martini a bit.'

'Your husband?' the bartender asked.

'Oh, he's not my husband. He's my husband's banker.' The bartender laughed, and I ordered another ginger ale.

7

We talked, they kept drinking, and Sadie and Eduard seemed to be hitting it off. Occasionally Eduard's legs bumped against mine. At first I didn't think it was intentional. The bar was getting too crowded.

'Would you like a hamburger?' I asked Eduard. 'Sadie says they're good.'

'The burgers?' Sadie yelled. 'They're great! The burgers are great. Brett, do you think they have buffalo wings? Eduard, how about you and me split a dozen wings? And chips and salsa! How come Mexico is the only place you can't get chips and salsa?'

'I'm sorry. Our kitchen is closed,' the bartender said. He had just served a final round of drinks.

'We'll take two burgers and a dozen wings!' Sadie said. 'Those are great burgers. Delicious! Where'd you get the cows?'

'Apparently we need some food,' I said to the bartender.

'If you go two blocks toward the water there's a place. Also, there's the Dino hotel, and they serve good pizza.'

Eduard took me by the wrist. 'Doesn't

pizza sound fantastic? Hawaiian pizza, that's what I want.' He swallowed half of his drink, paused, and then swallowed the other half. Sadie was almost at the bottom of her martini. I had lost track of their drinks. I'd had four or five ginger ales.

'Yeah, pizza!' Sadie said. She grabbed Eduard around the waist. He put one arm around her shoulders, and lay the other on mine. He was almost a foot taller than either of us. I could have fit under his chin.

'You're drunk,' I said.

For an hour or so, I had been worried because I thought, if he is flirting with me, I'm enjoying it. But now I decided it was alright. He was flirting with both of us, but it was innocent.

'Let's go, let's go,' Sadie said. It was pouring rain. We walked up the cobblestoned street, swaying and laughing, getting soaked. 'Pizza man!' Sadie shouted. 'Pizza man! Hey put that dog on a leash!'

A woman and man walking under a giant umbrella turned to look at us, startled. Sadie pointed across the street to an old, distinguished-looking man in a yellow rain-coat and wide-brimmed hat, and his wet, carefully-groomed white poodle. The dog was walking beside him and they both seemed not to notice the rain. Three tough-looking guys on the corner stood under a tattered awning, watching us. They had beers in their hands. Sadie slipped on a heel and Eduard caught her and almost fell, pulling me down as well. The three men laughed, and I saw it was okay.

But the restaurant at the hotel was closed, and so was the little place across the street with bars on the windows. All of the garage doors were pulled down across the businesses, the streets were empty except for us and the billboards for concrete companies and auto part stores, and I thought, 'Maybe they will go home together. How am I going to get a car?'

Eduard said, 'What about your hotel? Or mine? You're at the Ritz-Carleton, right? It must have a restaurant. You're the hotel expert.'

'It's half an hour from here,' I said. 'If we can find a cab.'

'I've got my car,' Eduard said.

'She's got the Presidential suite!' Sadie said. 'I'm staying there too. But her room is like a palace. And it's got this oversize minibar too, so you can eat all you want. You can eat anything! Plus, free booze!'

'Sound good?' Eduard asked me.

I thought, well, they'll eat, and then they'll go to bed.

8

Eduard and I were sitting on the red leather sofa and Sadie was in the chair next to the minibar. They had finished their steaks and were picking at their salads. I was exhausted. Sadie didn't want to leave, and Eduard was still talking and drinking. They both had booze energy. The party's over, I thought. I went to the bathroom and saw that Paul had called six times. He does not have a cell phone — he hates technology — and so I didn't return his call: I didn't like to imagine our home phones waking up his boys, and particularly Paul's father, who, when he had been drinking, would crawl into Paul's bed in his pajamas.

When I sat down Sadie opened the minibar again. She reached across Eduard's lap to refill his drink, allowing her shirt to fall open. She looked up at him and dropped her hand onto his leg. Eduard stood suddenly and went to the bathroom.

Sadie sat upright. She said, 'I think I'll go down to my room.'

'Please,' I said, 'it's late. Just stay here in my place tonight.' She gave me an angry look.

'Sadie,' I said, 'this is ridiculous. There's three bedrooms in this suite, I think. Or just sleep in bed with me.'

At that point I still meant everything I was saying. At least, I'm pretty sure I did.

She was already walking to the door. She stopped, turned, and looked at me for a moment when I said that, and I realized she was furious. I let her go. I sat and watched the ice melting in Eduard's whiskey and Sadie's vodka and almost picked one of them up to finish it. Then I realized, that's how tired you are. It had been two years, almost to the day, since I'd had a drink.

Eduard came out of the bathroom. 'Sadie left?'

'Yes. Jesus Christ. I'm sorry. I didn't expect her to get so drunk. We didn't get to talk. You're flying out tomorrow?'

'I think so,' he said. 'Who knows.' He put more ice in his drink and gestured at the window. The rain was going sideways. Up the beach in the lights from another resort you could see the palm trees bending almost to the ground. 'Don't you want one?' he asked.

'One what?' I knew what he meant.

'A drink. I don't care if you have one. Have one.' His smile was unexpected. He knew about my alcoholism. He said he'd read my novel, and even if he hadn't, in the old days

Paul had loved to complain to his friends about my drinking. I hesitated.

'Don't ever offer me a drink,' I said. 'I mean, I can't.'

'I just thought, you know, one. It doesn't do any harm.'

'Yeah,' I said. I didn't say anything else about that.

He took a couple sips of his drink and asked, 'Do you want to watch a movie?'

He got up and walked into the bedroom, where the TV was. From there he said, 'It's cold in here. Let's get under the covers.'

You always want a man to say that to you but they never do. When I'd stopped drinking I stopped behaving this way and I thought it was behind me. As I got into bed with him, I was still thinking, this is not the kind of thing that I do. He took the back of my head with one hand, and my throat and the base of my chin with the other. He kissed me.

When we stopped kissing, a long time later, I said, 'Eduard, I'm happily married.'

'I know,' he said.

We had sex until dawn. The storm had blown south and the sun was over the sea. We had sex at least seven times. An hour or so into it he told me that his girlfriend didn't like sex, and I was determined to make an impression.

21

9

'It's only three nights, Brett. He's our lifeline. We need him.'

'No, that's not what I'm saying. I want to meet him. I'm glad he's coming. I understand. It's just that I am barely back from Cancun. And now you've invited a friend to stay. Not a friend. Your banker.'

'Brett, it's not like I called him up. He has an appointment in town with Sergio.'

Sergio was one of Eduard's partners, and he handled all of our personal banking. He actually looked like I remembered Eduard looking.

'It's business. I don't want him to stay in a hotel. It'd be different if we had a property here. It's only polite.'

'Right.'

'Can I ask you, what is your problem with Eduard?'

'I don't have any problem, it just seems a bit odd to have him staying in our home. Did he ask to stay with us?'

Eduard and I had been talking on the phone almost every night. He texted me during the day. We wrote long emails.

It had snuck up on me. He'd come down

to our hotel in Tulum after the weekend with Sadie in Cancun.

It should have been a one-night thing, but we had both become fanatical at the same time. I was amazed at my own weakness.

'I told you. I invited him to stay here.'

'A week?'

'I couldn't exactly tell him how long he's allowed to stay.'

'Your dad's going to be in town at the same time. It's not going to be very nice for him. He wants all of us to spend time together.'

'My dad can't expect us to drop everything every time he comes to town. He doesn't expect us to.'

'Whatever. I'm just asking for a bit of help.'

'You're asking for a bit of help.'

'I don't like your tone, Paul.'

'I've had the kids all by myself for weeks, and you don't like my tone.'

I didn't remind him that the whole time I'd been gone, I was checking on our hotels. I didn't say he'd had Bella, his mom and his eldest son helping him, but I thought it. The more in the wrong I was, the easier it was for me to feel indignant. But I knew I was not in a position of leverage.

And of course I wanted Eduard to stay at our house.

'You're supposed to be off work for at least

a few days. It's Christmas. I don't know why he has to come during the holiday. It's just not considerate.'

'I don't set his schedule, Brett. Jesus. You know the position we're in. This is all part of expanding our properties. I mean, we're a bit stretched, honestly. The last thing we need to do right now is piss off the money guys.'

We had bought several hotels in resort locations a year before — some in excellent condition, some a mess — and we were still deep in renovations on a big place in Guatemala and a beachfront place in Panama. Paul's family had lots of money, but Paul had to make his own living, naturally.

'We have plenty of money,' I said. 'We can live on the income from your trusts if we just turn over Los Imperealos. Just sell it as is. Or let's have a party and bring some private people in. That's what your mom did. She always says private investors are the only good investors. Let's find a few angels.'

'I'm not ready for this fight again,' Paul said. 'I promise while he's in town I will make time to be home. I wish he weren't coming. Nobody wishes that more than I do. And Bella can take care of all the meals — or we'll go out.'

'No,' I said, 'have it your way, Paul. If he's coming, he's coming. We'll do it properly.'

10

I'd lived in Mexico for twelve years, but I had never made love to a Mexican man before. Most of the other ex-pats of a certain age had affairs with young Mexican men and I thought it was obvious and humiliating. 'Toreador,' Viola called hers; Becky's nickname for her current was 'Rabbit.' I tried 'The Goat' on Eduard but it never stuck. His name was always Eduard. His features were masculine: he had rough skin around his cheeks, his shoulders were wide but round, and he was not muscled but he was beautifully shaped and he was tall. He had been a boxer when he was in high school and college, and sometimes he'd stand on the bed and use my arms from behind to show me how to throw punches. He was awkward though and I knew many of my friends would be surprised if they knew. On the outside there was something about the two of us, if you looked at us, that didn't quite fit. But he would stop in windows and hold me and say: 'Now that's a beautiful couple' or 'Look at the young lovers' and kiss me. He could hold me by the back of the neck and toss me like a puppy. When he wore one of his suits and it was the cocktail hour and he took his first drink, my stomach turned, even after I knew him a year.

We could talk on the phone for five hours. One morning we started talking at just after eight and didn't get off the phone until he had to go home at six my time. He asked unexpected questions that made me see everything from a perspective that I had not imagined before. It sounds insincere, but he worried about Paul and the boys. One night, on the phone with him, in the car on the way back from the grocery store, I broke down crying and said, 'I'm a terrible wife, I'm not a good person. I'm as bad as everyone says.' He said, 'Don't flatter yourself. You're no better and no worse than anyone else.'

Sometimes, after we'd had an argument, he'd leave the hotel room and come back with a cut cheek, bruised ribs or a split lip. He was a grown man but he'd go get in a street brawl, in his suit and tie. I was never physically afraid of him. He was the most intimate lover I've ever had. 'I listen to you,' he'd tell me, when I asked him how he knew to do the things he did.

11

He didn't believe me when I told him I had a past.

'Well, I won't let you read my new book,' I said. It was a book I had been working on for five years, and would never finish. 'You'll think I slept with half of New York, and every able-bodied cowboy in Texas. Of course those were my drinking days. Most of that was before I met Paul. I mean it was all before Paul. Or before Paul and I were serious. There was one guy, a lawyer. I forget his name. This was a decade ago. He was a friend of Paul's. We were out at lunch, and when Paul left the table, I told him we should have a French affair. I suggested we meet in the afternoons for sex.'

'Sounds like a good deal for him.' Eduard didn't like to hear about my former lovers. But I didn't care. It wasn't a casual affair and I wanted him to know me.

'He wanted to meet at his apartment. He was too cheap to pay for a hotel. I stood outside of his building for nearly an hour, sweating in the sun, wearing a new dress and these stupid Chanel sunglasses — '

'I love those sunglasses.'

'Well, I finally called him. He didn't answer. Then I got a text message. It said, 'I forgot this is my laundry day. I only get one day a week to do laundry. Maybe next week?''

'I don't believe you.'

'That was the text. Word for word.'

'Did you meet with him the next week?' I bit him on the shoulder.

'You honestly think I would meet with him after that?'

'I don't even know why I'm asking. I don't want to know.'

'He was astonishing. He had a whole toolbox. It was better than a porn movie.' I said it with a straight face. The truth was I'd introduced that guy to YouPorn and Red-Tube. It took me a while to convince Eduard I was joking.

I said, 'All women over twenty-seven are whores.' Of course I might have just been talking about myself.

12

I was chubby as a kid. My mother told me, 'Don't worry, your time will come.' Once, on an airplane, flying to Copenhagen where my grandmother is from, a handsome man sitting beside me spread a blanket across my legs and his own. My mom was asleep right next to me. Everyone had their chairs all the way back. I had closed my eyes. The man slipped his hand under the blanket onto my knee, and then slowly worked up to my thigh. I was wearing jeans and after fifteen minutes or so with his hand between my legs, he unbuttoned them.

'Did you come?' Eduard asked me. 'How old were you? How old was he?'

'Oh this was just like, maybe ten years ago,' I said. I knew he had pictured me as fifteen or sixteen in the story. 'He was about your age, I'd guess. He had a beard and a nice tan. He had wrinkles at the corners of his eyes.'

'Did he ask for your number? Did he say anything? He must have known you were awake.'

'No, he just pretended like nothing had happened. I watched him get off the plane. I waited for him to look back.'

'Why wouldn't he?'

'He didn't,' I said. 'Of course.'

I did not tell him about the time I was in London on my first book tour. I had been drinking and I was unhappy. It was after the dinner and after the event following the dinner, and I had expected the guy I'd talked to all night to try to take me home, and he didn't, and I wanted to say, 'Let's just go back to your place,' because I think he was too shy to ask. So I went to a bar afterward and when some guys started acting weird, aggressive, I walked to a different bar. But I met a man on the street. He was American. He came up to me and said, 'I'll give you fifty pounds to suck my cock.' He had been drinking too. He was handsome and I went to my knees. He couldn't come, and I started to give up. Then he took me by my hair and one arm and pulled me into an alleyway. He pushed me over a trashcan, pushed up my dress and pulled down my panties.

'I didn't say you could fuck me,' I said. 'You shouldn't be doing it like this.'

He said, 'You're right,' and raped me in the ass.

There are a lot of stories like that. Once I begin, I want to tell them all. Sitting here in a small, borrowed room in Galveston, I want to

30

forget the whole history of Brett and Eduard and tell each and every one of my other love stories and sex stories and lies. But there are things I can never tell anybody.

13

'I have most of what we need,' I said. I was making dinner for Eduard, who had arrived that morning. It was a warm day. I had the windows in the kitchen open and you could smell the flowers from the courtyard, the wet flagstones and our big cypress trees.

'But what don't you have?' Paul asked. He took a handful of grapes, and Eduard stood in the doorway to the kitchen. He wore a T-shirt and a pair of dark jeans.

'Some onions and carrots, a leek, two bottles of red wine, and something for everyone to drink. Some limes for your dad? Gatorade if they have some, and maybe tonic water.'

Paul and Eduard went to the grocery store. I hadn't been able to look straight at Eduard yet. If I could drink it would be easier. I broke down and went up to the medicine cabinet for some of Paul's father's Klonopins. I took three, which might have been too many. When Paul came back half an hour later, I was relaxed. He put the bags on the counter and put his arms around me and kissed the nape of my neck. I said, 'Where's Eduard?'

'He's in the car,' he said. 'I remembered egg noodles and thyme.'

'Why doesn't he come in?'

'I invited him to the races. Also I think he picked up on your feelings about his visit. He said he would switch to a hotel.'

'That's crazy. Should I go out and get him?'

'No, let's just leave him alone.' I didn't know whether or not Paul had any suspicions about me and Eduard but I complained about him as often as I could.

'He is high maintenance. No more weeklong visits for Eduard.'

'He just got here, for crying out loud.'

'You haven't been cooking the past five hours.'

'I'm sorry. It's just because he doesn't have kids. He's practically a kid himself. He has to be entertained all the time. Speaking of. I'm late.'

'You forgot the wine.'

'Shit. I did. Do you need me to go out again and get it?'

'Well, yeah.'

'Okay, it's just that we'll be late.'

'I don't want to interrupt the boys' games with the ingredients for their dinner. I don't want to have to pack them up and drag them out with me.'

He kissed my forehead. 'I'll go.'

I knew that I could get the wine while his dad watched the kids. Or his dad could get it. Or the kids and I could get it. But for some reason I felt indignant.

I didn't think, Well, after all, I'm making dinner for my lover, who is staying in our home. Or, if I did think that, I thought as quickly, 'There is no way for Paul to know that.'

I said, 'I'm sorry, but I can't make a daube without wine.'

Later Eduard often told me: 'That day with the wine, when Paul and I had to make two trips. That's when I knew you were in the wrong relationship.'

14

'Say what you like about the Mexicans, those Mexican mothers are doing something right — seems like every Mexican you introduce me to is a doctor, a lawyer, a banker — that doesn't happen by accident. That's a good upbringing. Nurturing.'

He looked over his shoulder at Paul's sons, who were eating at the coffee table and watching a show on the computer, and then he gave me a pointed look. Paul's dad had been pouring his own drinks. He took a sip of his Glenlivet and started again.

'These Mexicans have done a lot more good than you might think. Think about their environment. How do you survive in the desert?'

'Camels,' Eduard said. He had been drinking too. I did not like his expression.

Paul's father laughed. 'Ok, Eduard, your forefathers are in the desert, getting chased by the Spanish, by Christians, Americans, the Texans, so they needed transportable money. Paul, you know this one.'

'Diamonds?' Eduard said. 'Gold? Mayan gold?'

'Conquistadors, sure. But that was their problem, really, not the solution. Think bigger now. Think the twin towers.'

'The twin towers?' I said.

'Surely you don't mean drugs. Drugs and terrorism?' Paul lifted his fork. 'Dad — '

'Banking! They're taking over the banks! Right, Eduard? And what's banking? Interest! They're Catholics, sure, but according to the Mexicans making money is a virtue. That's the truth. All through Central America, in fact. That's why the Communists could never get a foothold here, the way they have in South America. It's in their blood. Eduard, back me up here. I heard it from my own banker. He's Honduran and about as good a guy as you ever met. Of course the drug trade has had its impact. Money laundering. That's how the banking originally shifted south. We've got the drug wars to thank for that. Any war you ever heard of, there's a plus side, even for us pacifists. You can't get interest in American banks any more. But the Mexicans figured it all out. Am I right, Eduard? When you think about it, you give a man a dollar and he gives you a dollar and a half back. That's genius. That's pure genius.'

I'd had enough. I said, 'So how long have you been dating your girlfriend, Eduard? She's a banker too?'

'She's a counselor. A kind of psychiatrist. She works with drug-addicted teens.'

'Pure Latin American genius! That's the twin towers connection. Banking in America is dead.'

'I guess we've been together six years now?' Eduard looked confused. 'We met when one of my partners was having problems with his son. A heroin problem. That's the real drug problem in this part of the world. The kids.'

'It's true, that's the unintended consequence,' Paul's father said.

'There's no such thing as a free lunch, Eduard.'

'I've told you about her,' Paul said. He was getting upset. 'Her name is Lurisia.'

'She's a very beautiful woman,' I said. I'd been looking at pictures of Lurisia on Facebook. 'She's a swimmer. She's Castilian.'

'Have you met her?' Paul asked me. 'When did you meet Lurisia?'

Paul's dad gave me a curious, sarcastic look. He thought I was always cheating on Paul.

'She also works in an abortion clinic,' Eduard said. 'To tell you the truth, I don't approve of that.'

'Come on, Eduard,' Paul's father said. 'You're behind the times. A woman should have as much control over her body as a man. The government doesn't tell you what to do with your cock. They don't tell you to meet with the Feds before you get a vasectomy.'

'Dad!' Paul said.

'I don't know,' Eduard said. 'Perhaps a man should have to meet with a psychologist before a vasectomy.'

'You're not thinking it through, Eduard. Suppose you were hooked up to a famous violinist,' Paul's dad said. 'And they told you you'd be breaking the law unless you stayed in the hospital for nine months.'

'Say again?'

'Paul,' I said.

'The violinist dies unless your livers are connected. You have to be in bed with the world's best violinist for nine months.'

'Man or a woman?' Eduard asked. I left the table and went to play with Paul's sons.

★   ★   ★

After dessert Eduard came to sit with us and offered to read the boys a book. He had brought books for them and Paul's six-year-old sat in his lap. He read well, and he turned the pages. He offered to read them to sleep. I said, 'No, I'll do that.'

Paul said, 'No, let me.'

Putting the kids to bed was something Paul did.

I went to the kitchen to wash the dishes. I heard Paul's dad say behind me, to Eduard, 'Those kids just prefer men. You're good with them. I think they scare her. 'Course not everybody's cut out to be a stepmother.'

'Can I refill your drink, Don?'

'Why thank you, Eduard. I believe this soldier is dead.'

The man has drunk an entire bottle of scotch by himself, I thought.

Eduard came up behind me. He kissed the back of my neck. 'Let's go out,' he said.

'You're crazy.'

'Don't worry. These two are easy. I'll go talk to Paul. You get ready.'

15

We went to the bar at The Raphael Hotel on the plaza. A band was playing. Eduard was drinking whiskey and I had my Coke Light.

He leaned forward to kiss me and squirted whiskey into my mouth. 'Let's get a room,' Eduard said.

A lawyer type at the end of the bar was trying to catch my eye. Eduard went to the bathroom and the guy with the lawyer-look tried to talk to me, telling me his name. 'Are you visiting Mexico City? Do you like the Zócalo?'

When Eduard came back I had brushed him off but he was still looking. Eduard stared him down.

'Do you see that guy?' he asked.

'Yes. He introduced himself to me when you were in the bathroom. He's a real estate developer.'

'My father was a real estate developer. I know about real estate developers.'

'Hi,' Eduard said to the man, who was about fifty and handsome.

His suit was expensive. I looked at his shoes. The same.

He introduced himself to Eduard. They shook hands. Eduard smiled at him warmly. I watched them both look at each other with confidence.

'Ok,' Eduard said, and put his arm around my waist. I was still sitting. Eduard told the bartender a room number. He lifted me off the bar stool, and picked up his drink.

'Have a good night,' he said to the man, still smiling.

The real estate developer saw how easily and thoroughly he'd been beaten. He smiled thinly back at me and we both understood.

When Eduard got us to the elevator I turned and kissed him with my arms on his back and my hands reaching up for his shoulders. I pressed the whole length of my body against him.

'I liked that,' I said, and whispered into his ear. 'I'm sopping wet.'

We got home just before the sun rose. Paul's dad was on his back in bed next to him, in his clothes, his shoes still on, snoring. His hands were folded behind his head and one elbow was pressed against Paul's ear. I took a shower, made coffee, and fell asleep in a blanket with my head in my arms at the kitchen table.

16

The following afternoon, Eduard was beside me in my truck, driving. We were coming back to Mexico City after a trip into the country 'to look at a new property.' We'd brought one of Paul's sons along as cover. He was in the back seat, watching a movie on his iPad.

We wanted to be as close to each other as we could, and it was hard riding next to him and not being allowed to kiss his neck or his cheek or hold his wrist. We had a ten-year-old chaperone.

The rain never stopped. We were halfway back from Calderon, passing cars pulled over on the side of the road. Outside a mile-long maquiladora a jackknifed semi had flipped over on its side. The driver was standing beside his truck with rain coming down on his shoulders. We'd seen police cars, sand trucks, wet horses and collapsed huts on the wet highway. There was no sun, just low clouds and the rain.

Always, during our time together, it was sun or rain.

'So we're going home?'

'I think we'd better.' I glanced with my eyes

at the back seat. 'I'm ready to go home,' Paul's son said.

'It's not even five o'clock. Aren't you hungry, buddy?' Eduard smiled back at him. 'This is when civilized people have lunch.'

'We can stop and get something to eat if you want,' I said.

'I want to go home, Brett. I don't want to eat in a restaurant. I want to see daddy and grandpa. I'm bored.'

'Let's drop him off,' Eduard said. 'I'll run him in and tell Paul that I want you to meet some potential investors. He's got his dad to take care of. I'll tell him you'll sell the idea better than he can. Nobody can sell like a beautiful woman. He knows that.'

I gave Eduard a look: he's ten, for Christ's sake, he can understand every word you're saying. People who don't have children don't understand that they are smarter than adults.

'Brett, you can really help me close this deal,' he said loudly. 'I need your savvy on this one. This will help the hotels. This will really help Paul.'

I rolled down the window and let the rain blow into the jeep. 'You're getting us all wet!' Eduard said, and he laughed. Then all three of us laughed, we rolled down all our windows, and I was in love again, even more than two minutes before.

17

When we got to the restaurant Eduard pulled in front and I said, 'Can we park here?'

'Let's have a drink,' he said. He gave the valet my keys, and told him we'd be back shortly. 'Maybe we'll make it back in time to have dinner with them. Maybe we won't.'

I knew Paul's dad would be watching our time.

'We really need to be home tonight, Eduard. Paul trusts me. He's not a jealous person. But he isn't dumb.'

'I know, I know, I'm sorry,' he said. 'It's easier for me, because Lurisia stays so busy.'

I thought this was a veiled insult to Paul but I didn't say anything.

In the bar a band was playing. Eduard ordered a drink. My phone was buzzing in my purse and I turned it off without looking to see who it was. I was sick to my stomach from the drive and worrying about Paul and his dad. The set ended, and the drummer came to the bar and stood next to Eduard. She ordered a Hendrick's gin and tonic. Slice of cucumber. She was younger than me.

'You guys can play,' Eduard said to her.

She was too skinny, and her skin was pocked and covered in heavy makeup. I wasn't concerned.

'Thanks,' she said. 'We're playing at The Blue Note after this. Eleven o'clock session.'

Eduard looked at me. I looked at the drummer. I looked at her with his eyes, and I could see that she wasn't too bad.

'It's a great place,' I said.

'Come down. I'll buy you guys a drink. You're a beautiful couple.'

'She can't go,' Eduard said. 'She's too tired. She's going home.'

'On a Friday night? Well, that's okay. A woman needs her beauty sleep. You can come alone, if you want. Don't worry, señora, I'll show the proper respect.' She patted me on the shoulder, reaching over Eduard.

Eduard told the bartender he would buy her drink.

'No no, thank you very much, but my drinks are on the house. What do you drink?'

'She drinks Coke Light,' Eduard said. 'I'll have a Jameson's. Not too much ice. You really shouldn't. But thank you.'

'A Coke Light,' she laughed. 'And a Jameson's Irish whiskey for the gentleman please, Bobby. One cube of ice.' The drummer told us her name was Maxine, but asked us to call her Max. She gave me a card.

Maxine Groove. You can look her up in Mexico City, that's her real stage name.

'That's exactly how I like it,' Eduard said about his whiskey. 'How did you know?'

All this time I had been filling his glass with ice. Maxine stepped away to go to the bathroom.

'You're seriously going to the Jazz District with that girl?'

'Well, I have the night in Mexico City, I'm not just going to sit in your house.'

'I — ' There was nothing I could say. 'Drink your drink,' I said. When Max came back I told her we'd see her down at the club.

'I'm glad to hear you changed your mind,' she said. 'How's the Coke Light?'

They started to play again. I told Eduard there was a much better club I wanted him to see, where they opened at midnight and played until sunrise.

'Listen,' he said. 'After my drink we'll get a room. The Four Seasons is five minutes from here. We can order some room service if you're hungry.' I was hoping he'd have another drink, get sleepy, and want to go home. This was before I understood he was inexhaustible. He said, 'Then we'll go hear some real music. I hate jazz. Did you see that Maxine? What a slut.'

I understood that by not going home I was

making another small bad real decision, like I had made when I climbed into bed with him that first night.

All these decisions you make for the sake of your lover are little steps you take away from the person you truly love. That's not to say you don't love them both, you do. But one has your heart and the other has your attention.

Then, after many little steps, you turn around and he's so far away that you think, well, he's too far away now. We've gone.

18

Up in the room, I went into the bathroom to call Paul. When I came out, there was a silver tray on the bed with two hamburgers, french fries, a rose, three whiskies and three Coke Lights. Eduard was sitting on the edge of the bed with his shoes off and his back to me, looking out at the city. I lay down next to him. He didn't move, so I touched his belt loop.

'You got room service.'

He took a drink then turned and grabbed my head with both his hands and kissed me, his mouth full of whiskey. I took one of his hands from my head and put it between my legs.

19

A little past three in the morning, I went to the minibar and poured myself a vodka. It was the first drink I'd taken in two years. I savored it. Then I had several more. They woke me and my spine tingled. Dangerously close to sunrise, I woke Eduard, and told him we had to go. Eduard carried me to the truck. He stumbled and nearly dropped me. 'I can walk!' I said, laughing. We sat in the truck with the heat blowing and the seat warmers on and kissed. 'Let's go back inside the hotel,' he said.

'Eduard. Paul.'

He drove carefully, because of the wet streets and the whiskey.

My vodka had had a disappointing effect on me. There was no happy glow like I remembered and expected.

20

When we got home Paul's dad was still up, drinking.

'How'd it go with the investors?' He leered at us. 'How's the investors? How's the investors, Brett?'

'Go to bed, Don,' I said.

'Here, I'll take him,' Eduard said.

'I can find my own goddamn bed in this house! This is my son's house! My son!'

I said, 'You're going to wake the boys, Don.' I was worried about Paul.

'Here, let's have a drink, Don,' Eduard said. 'Let's have a drink and talk. I think you've got something on your mind.' He turned to me. 'Why don't you check on the boys, Brett?'

I went to see that Paul was still asleep. Then I made myself a whiskey and went to the guest room to wait for Eduard. I chose whiskey because I wanted Eduard to taste himself on my breath. I knew Paul's dad would end up in our bed again, asleep with his son.

21

Eduard woke me up when he came in.

'He's asleep,' he said. 'Don't worry, they're all asleep.'

We made love very gently. I couldn't come, because of all the booze, but I didn't pretend, and he didn't mind.

We lay there and talked. I felt like I could coil up on his belly.

That first drunk when you haven't been drunk in a long time is not really fun. But you recover parts of your personality you'd forgotten, or that had fallen asleep, or were even no longer there.

'You didn't come. Let's make love again.'

I don't know why I was suddenly angry with him. But I wanted to hurt him.

'The thing is, you know, Paul, he has. Well, you know what I'm going to say.'

He didn't know what I was going to say.

'He has, you know, a big cock. Really big, actually. It's a beautiful cock too. I mean, it's like you think a cock ought to look.'

'Like a what's-his-name cock.'

'Mapplethorpe.'

'Yeah, okay, I got it.'

I touched his face and regretted what I'd told him.

'Don't get me wrong, that's not what I'm saying. I love your cock. In fact, his cock just hurts.'

The truth is, I don't know why I said it. Maybe I was trying to be truthful. But he said it didn't bother him. He told me a similar thing happened to him once, when he was with a woman in a movie theater. The movie was about Henry Miller and Anais Nin, and at one point Nin tells Miller, about a rival, 'I like your cock better. His is too big.'

Eduard told me, 'The girl I was with at the movie said, about her husband, 'That's just how I feel. I really like your cock much better than his.''

'Exactly,' I said. 'That's how I feel too.' I didn't care one way or the other. Though I remembered that when Paul and I first met, I thought his soul-destroying cock meant we were supposed to be together.

Eduard liked to choke me or gag me with his hand while we fucked. He also liked to slap me, hard, in the face and on my breasts, and especially on my legs and ass.

I never told him that I needed him to do these things to me. He intuited it.

'It even scares me,' he said, 'how violent our sex is.' I said, 'I don't believe you.'

Often while walking to the library, or shopping in Palanco, the women I didn't know pulled me aside on the street to ask: 'Is everything alright? Can I help?' I enjoyed that.

22

'Hey, I have good news.'

'What is it?'

I was excited. I thought Eduard meant good news about us.

'My partners liked Paul's pitch. They're giving him the financing for the property in Costa Rica.'

'Oh, okay.'

'Don't sound too thrilled.'

'I'm glad we got the money. But if Paul's going to Costa Rica all the time, then so are you. And I'm going to be stuck here with the boys. We don't need any more goddamn hotels. We have plenty of money. Tell me you're building a new property in Mexico City and I'll be happy.'

'I'll call them back and kill the deal.'

'Thank you.'

'I'll tell them I can't fuck Paul's wife like she needs it unless we build a resort next to his house.'

'Oh you know . . . ' I hung up the phone before I said it. 'Fuck you, Eduard.'

23

He was the first man I ever met who, when we were about ten feet away from each another, I could feel a force pulling us together, like there was an electrical circuit that must be completed. When we left each other I could sense its resistance. 'Can you feel that?' I'd sometimes ask him, and he'd say, 'Of course.' Then when it broke there was both loneliness and this elated, dizzy certainty of liberation.

I worried that we brought out the worst in each other.

It's very hard to know, in the early few months of a love affair, what is real and what is imaginary. You find signs and confirmations everywhere. Men passing you on the street stop you to tell you that you're beautiful. Random street signs or airplanes passing overhead prophesize your happiness.

Yet the mind of your lover remains as closed to you as that of a face on a billboard, or a distracted cab driver fiddling with his radio.

Every time I looked at him, when we were happy together, I wanted to put him entirely in my mouth.

24

I'd agreed to do a reading in Miami in order to meet Eduard. I was in a Starbuck's in South Beach arguing with Paul on the phone. He was finally having suspicions.

'I can't just get on a plane and come home,' I said. 'You know I hate Miami. You know how much I hate readings.'

'You say you hate readings but then why are you there? Fine. Come home right after. Get a late flight out tonight.'

'I'm going out to dinner with my agent tomorrow. It's a big deal, Paul. It's my career. People are forgetting I exist. I'm a writer. I don't manage hotels.'

Paul hung up the phone. I tried to call him back three times, but he had taken it off the hook. I called Bella on her cell and asked her if she could get Paul, but she wasn't at the house.

A handsome Swedish man who had been watching me from the corner of the Starbuck's said, 'Are you alright?'

'Are you married?'

'No,' he said, and smiled.

'Don't,' I said. 'I've tried it twice now.'

56

25

Sadie had insisted on flying to Miami to meet me. She had a condo in Coral Gables. I didn't want her to come. I should never have mentioned it to her.

During an affair you need your closest friends, because you are falling apart, but then they try to fix things, which is what you don't want them to do. I was asking her to help me stop seeing Eduard but I couldn't stop seeing Eduard.

'Someone's got to keep an eye on you,' she said.

'You're one to talk.'

'I sleep with guys, I don't fall in love with them.'

'Sadie, I'm not joking. I have to meet my agent, and when I'm not with her I'll be with Eduard. You know I'd love to see you. But I don't see how we'll even spend any time together.'

'You stood me up when we were in Cancun. We could have had a perfectly good three-way and none of this would have happened. But you had to kick me out of your room and now your whole life is fucked.

You're not going to do it this time. You asked me to come.'

'Sadie, I didn't invite you to Miami.'

'Yes you did.'

'What?' I didn't know whether or not I'd invited her. But now I was uninviting her.

'I'm looking up flights right now — if I get on — okay, see you in five hours.'

26

I met Sadie at her husband's club. I told the doorman I was meeting Mrs. Brauer. He showed me to a tall, elegantly dressed Cuban man with round glasses whose job was to stand behind an enormous desk, who showed me to the maître d', who gave me to a waiter, who took me to her table. She was sitting on a richly upholstered sofa with Swarovski lamps on both sides and a marble-topped Louis Quinze table in front of it.

I kept checking my phone for texts from Eduard. I was trying not to text him.

When I saw Sadie at her table in a cream Van Laack dress, with Celine heels and the open smile of a friend who loves you, I wanted to move to Miami and forget about Eduard, Paul and his children, and my whole life in Mexico City. But I was in love with Eduard, and I loved my husband and his boys, and Sadie ordered Coke Lights for us both.

'Why aren't you drinking wine?' I said. 'I'm not in the mood.'

Sadie ordered us a charcuterie. I ordered her a glass of white wine.

She said, 'Brett. You don't look good.'

'Thanks.'

'Are you drinking with him?' I lifted a shoulder. I was about to cry.

She said, 'Oof. Are you writing? What's going on with Paul?'

'I'm writing,' I lied. Then I said, 'I wrote a page. Shit, I don't know.' There was a black businessman at the table behind ours. He kept catching my eye and I wondered why. Then I thought, it's because he thinks I'm staring at him.

'I'm not drinking,' I said. 'It's not like that at all. It has nothing to do with drinking or writing.'

Sadie was my friend, but she didn't need to be lecturing me. I said, 'Imagine if you had a problem. Some kind of problem. Let's say it was your weight. And sometimes you had a handle on it and sometimes you didn't, and everywhere you went, everyone you met, man, woman and child, counseled you on it. Counseled, advised, or questioned you on it. I always want to tell people: I quit drinking and writing at the same time. Funny coincidence. But I never have to. Before I bring it up they always deny the connection, because everybody knows: I drink, I hurt myself and the people around me, and then I write.'

I was shaking. I stood up.

'Honey. Sit down. I'm sorry. It's alright. Does Paul know?' Sadie said.

'About my drinking? Of course not. Sadie. No. God forbid.' I sat down. 'He'd have already checked me into the hospital.'

'No, dummy. About Eduard.' I started to laugh. I thought, if I sit here even five minutes longer, I'm going to order myself a drink, whether Sadie wants one or not.

27

After the reading, at the reception, Eduard told me he had brought Lurisia to Miami.

'She insisted at the last minute.'

'What? Is she here?' I looked around. It was a charity reading hosted by the Tiffany Circle, and hundreds of people were there.

'No, of course not, I would never do that. She's at the hotel.'

'Ok, fine. You're still staying with me. I don't care what you have to do.' I would make him pay for this later. 'I want to meet her,' I said.

'Well, it'd be a little awkward if not.'

It was so outrageous that I became very calm. I thought, Okay, Eduard.

I'll stay this calm. I can handle it.

I said, 'When?'

'We're all going for drinks with a couple of clients after.'

'With clients of yours?'

'So you want it to be just the three of us?' He smiled with one side of his mouth and said, 'I'll make it fun. I'll sit by you. I had to put up with Paul for a whole week, Brett.'

'You invited yourself!'

I looked around and lowered my voice.

'You're staying with me tonight.'

'Fine. I mean, yes. Of course. I don't know how exactly. But yes, it's a deal.'

I signed copies of a book I'd written three years before, and Eduard and Sadie chatted. Afterwards we asked her to come with us to meet Lurisia and Eduard's clients, Sadie looked at Eduard and said, with no expression in her voice, 'Oh no, I'm exhausted.'

The truth is, although I needed her there, I didn't want her to come.

In the taxi, Eduard said he wanted to stop at my hotel before meeting everyone at the bar.

'We don't have time.'

'I don't care,' he said, and looked at his watch. 'Okay, Brett, you're right, we're keeping everyone waiting.'

Eduard tried to stop me, but I gave him a blowjob while the driver, a Sikh in a blue turban, kept his eyes on the road.

Eduard's clients were married. One was a prominent architect, and the other was an English indie actress I'd seen in a couple of movies from five or six years ago. They were between my age and his. The woman, who was the more attractive and successful of the two, flirted with Eduard. Lurisia just sat there and took it. I put my foot on Eduard's leg under the table, and the actresses's husband started to flirt with me. No one was flirting with Lurisia and she didn't seem to notice. She was one of those naturally happy people. I don't know whether or not Eduard had told Lurisia we were involved. She looked at me like she knew. I wasn't hiding anything from anyone.

The waiter brought our drinks. He poured my near-beer from high above the glass. I knew how difficult it was to pour a beer like that without foaming it over. I also understood that the waiter was trying to console me for being the only one not drinking. Pouring it like that made it seem like a nice drink.

'That was an elegant pour,' I said, and the waiter smiled.

We took two cabs to the party. I made a point of riding with Lurisia. She was an impeccable dresser, with intelligent and sensitive eyes, and we complained about the shopping in Miami. Eduard rode with the actress and the architect.

At the party Eduard took me by the arm and said, '"An elegant pour?" What was that?'

'What are you talking about? The waiter?'

'Yes, Brett.'

'He did a nice job of pouring the beer.'

'An elegant job. On his pour. My clients thought you were coming on to him.'

64

'I'd say it again. He was pouring it that way deliberately. It's not as easy as it looks.'

'People don't say things like that to service people, Brett. It was tacky. My friends thought you were coming on to him.'

'You don't know what you're talking about, Eduard.' Then I said, 'I'm surrounded by savages.'

'What?'

'Nothing.'

'I heard what you said, Brett.'

'You mean, when I called you a savage?'

I was getting very angry.

'Yeah, I'm the savage,' he said. 'That's priceless.'

'A fucking wetback savage.'

After I said it I was afraid he'd walk away. But then I saw from his expression that he was afraid I would walk away, and suddenly he didn't look handsome and fearsome. He looked confused, like he didn't know what to do. He looked like a little kid, and I wished I could hold him. He took a sip of his drink, still facing the bookshelves of the apartment we were in, and I fell in love with him again. I reached out and took his fingers in my hand. We made up.

28

After the fight, Eduard sent Lurisia to a club with his clients, and spent the night at my hotel. The next morning when I was trying to leave for a meeting with my agent and my editor, he wouldn't stop fucking me. 'Stop. I really have to go!' I said, and I couldn't tell how much I meant it. There were often those moments when I meant it but I didn't. That was part of the reason he wouldn't let me out of the room. He wanted me to understand that he mattered more than my meeting did. That I needed him more than I would admit to myself.

I never felt that our sex had anything to do with control, though. It was about need, or about proving ourselves to each other.

Then he started to spank me with the palms of his hands and the backs of his hands. He had a boxer's break on the middle finger of his right hand and I could feel the knuckle every time he slapped me. The more I hurt the harder we fucked. He beat me. I'd had enough and tried to get up. He swore at me and threw me back down on the bed every time I rose. He pinned both my arms

66

behind my back and slapped me with his right hand. Then he slapped my face whichever way I turned it. I cried. 'No!' I screamed, and bit him. I drew blood on his shoulder. After the sex was over my ass was bleeding.

He said, 'You wouldn't believe what your ass looks like.'

'I think I have some idea.'

He took a picture with his phone. It was red and purple and there were lines of blood showing through my skin.

I said, 'That's my ass.'

29

The next night, I was with Eduard and Lurisia at another party. It was the after party for a wedding. Lines of coke were cut on the tables, and people were drinking guava mojitos. Eduard was embarrassed. He asked me: 'Do you mind if I do a line?'

There was a girl who wouldn't leave me alone. She was a writer for *Newsweek*. She kept telling me how much she'd loved my novel, and she wanted to write a story together on Mexican prisons. She said, 'I'm in with the warden in Guadalajara. We could spend the night.'

Paul called. He said, 'I feel like I'm going crazy.' He sounded like he had been crying.

'What do you mean?'

'I mean I'm losing my mind. I never talk to you anymore. You're never home. I don't think you care about me or the boys. When you're not writing you're off at one of the hotels, or talking on the phone. I never see you. I have to go to Costa Rica soon, and I can't count on you to take care of your own family. I feel like you're drinking again.'

'Our lives haven't changed,' I said. 'You

know your trip to Guatemala next weekend? Why don't the two of us go? You can leave the boys with your dad. We'll leave on Friday and come back Sunday or Monday. Just us.'

Paul said, 'You promise?'

I remembered that he was my husband, then, and that I loved him, and that I wanted to go back to him, to go home, to forget all this. You're a wife, Brett, I told myself. You can be a good wife. Paul deserves that. You need it.

I got off the phone and waved to Eduard. He was talking to another woman. A painter. A young girl with a mole on her left cheek, who had done an entire series of canvases with mud.

Eduard put his hand on her wrist and I gave up, came over, and put my arm around him. I didn't know where Lurisia was. He smiled at me.

'Are you ready?' I said. 'I think we better go.'

'Just a minute.' The girl with the mole introduced herself to me. I told her my name and she said, 'I know who you are! Of course.'

I hate those women who hurt you, and want to be your friend. But often I wish I could do that. Paul's mother was the master. She could say something nice to you that destroyed you for a week.

The bride appeared, back in her wedding dress, but with the bodice pulled down almost to her waist. She'd put her veil back on and she was dancing. Her tits were bouncing all over the place. Her husband said, 'Don't come out here like that.' She stood up on a coffee table, wobbling.

'I'm married! I'm married! Hey everybody, I am married!' She was waving her ring finger at the crowd. Someone shouted, 'You are dancing on the coke!'

The painter said to me, 'Pretty.'

Eduard said, 'Okay, you two.'

I gave him a ferocious look. I said to the painter, 'You should paint about it. You could do a whole cycle on tits.'

The painter said, 'You know, that's actually a really good idea.

It's funny you say that. I just sold a painting called 'Tits' in a gallery that represents me in L.A.'

At that point I gave up. I said to Eduard, 'Come and find me when you're ready to leave.'

30

I went to the bar and asked the bartender to pour me a club soda. Then I said, 'You know what, add a couple of fingers of vodka to that. Just float it on top. There, yes, a little more, thanks.'

I drank it standing there and got a second. 'Easy on the soda,' I told him.

31

Shortly before we met, Eduard had been in love with a singer from Brazil, and I knew he still was. He was in love with both of us, and probably with Lurisia. There were times when I was suffering, thinking about him with Lurisia or the Brazilian or some other woman he might have loved. I thought, I can't lie to him anymore about anything. I'm too tired. I wanted to beg him, can't I just abandon myself to you? Won't you simply take me as I am, exactly as I am, because I am giving myself entirely to you? But then I sensed the need, again, for pretense, if wanted to be attractive to him, if I wanted to be loved in return.

I tried to talk to him about it — and we could talk about those things — and he said he felt the same way. That could not have been a lie.

32

After Miami I got Paul out of Mexico City as quickly as I could. We were in bed at the Casas Santa Domingo, just outside Antigua. We'd made love twice that morning, and we were eating warm lobster pupusas in bed. There was coffee spilled on the sheets. Paul had asked for peonies in the room — my wedding bouquet was yellow peonies — and the torn-petaled flowers were everywhere. They'd even put a yellow peony on the silver breakfast tray instead of a rose.

'Do you remember Honduras?' Paul said.

I said, 'Do you know the most beautiful thing about this flower?'

'You told me but say it again.'

'It has so many petals that it can't open unless ants chew through the casing.'

We had a movie on. He had to leave to look at a new property in an hour. 'I think Honduras was our best vacation ever,' I said.

In Honduras we'd stayed for a week in the tiny Mayan town of Copan, high in the mountains. After a horse ride through the coffee fields we'd bathed in a hot spring — there were a dozen pools — that ran off a mountain stream. The stream itself was boiling: you couldn't touch it. Then a group of middle-aged Japanese women joined us in the deep rock pool. They bathed naked and didn't speak. I had the thought that my dead mother was there, smiling at us, approving. I imagined her thinking: 'At last my little lone wolf has figured it out.'

The sun set. We had no flashlight and we couldn't find our shoes. I held Paul's hand as we picked our way slowly down the path and across a swinging wooden bridge. Our hotel, a stone cabin that was part of an old plantation built on the ruins of a temple, was lit by dozens of candles. There was no electricity, the mountain air was cold, and there were piles of blankets at the foot of the bed. We only called to speak with Paul's sons and I didn't write or check email. There were no mosquitoes. We had been sober together for a long time and we did not want wine or margaritas. We tanned in the mountains, we were slender. He told me I had never been so beautiful. He had never been so beautiful. I understood, then, that he was the only man I'd ever loved, would ever love.

In the pictures from that time we are sitting so close together, so wrapped up, we could be one person with two heads and four arms and legs, like a Mayan idol.

He said, 'Along with our honeymoon, it was our most romantic vacation.'

'It feels like a long time ago. I'm tired, Paul.'

'Things will get easier soon. I'm opening the new properties. I've been working too much. I love you. Everything's going to be ok. We'll take another vacation soon. The boys are getting older. We could go to Argentina for a week.'

'Or Sri Lanka,' I said. 'Or Madagascar. Get off the continent altogether.'

We made love again.

When Paul got dressed and left to drive to the coast, I called Eduard. 'I miss you,' I said. 'What are you doing?'

'I miss you so much I feel sick. I can actually feel it.'

I was glad. 'I know. It's like someone's pulling on a wire that's tied up inside your chest. It hurts. I can talk for almost an hour. How long can you talk?'

The phone beeped. It was Paul. I ignored it.

'I can talk,' he said. 'Are you guys having fun? How's the hotel? I've always wanted to stay at that place.'

'I wish you were here. Paul's happy.'

'That's good. He deserves it.'

'I deserve to be fucking you. And I don't

want to have to wait another week before we are.'

When Paul came back from his meeting I was asleep. He got in bed beside me and told me about his ideas for the new hotel. He was excited about the bathtubs. 'They'll be carved out of quartz. I didn't even know that was possible. You'll be in the bath, outside, watching the sea. I'm so grateful we got away. Let's go to dinner. I'm going to keep my tie on. I want to be dressed up.'

He was so happy. I was miserable, and on the way back from the bathroom I ran to the room and drank two bottles of vodka from the minibar.

I kept having visions of Eduard, and I couldn't sleep. I was losing weight.

33

I was back in Mexico City at the university library working on my new novel. Sitting at the computer, I could feel that I hadn't been writing in a long time. But I had energy from being sad and being angry. It was coming back fast.

'That's your phone ringing,' the librarian said. 'Señora? Señora Ramsey? That's your phone.'

I jumped up, answered the call and headed for the stacks to talk, thinking it was Eduard.

It was Paul. He was talking very quickly, He said, 'Have you been talking to Eduard? About a new contract? Has Eduard been calling you about business? Is there some deal we're doing with Eduard that I don't know about? Is there a problem?' He was reaching for any possibility. 'Your cellphone bill is almost six hundred dollars. It's all calls to Eduard's number.'

'I'm coming home.' I hung up.

When I got there he was at the gate, smoking. He had the phone bill in his hands. It was the first time I had seen him smoking since he quit four years before, when the doctor told him that the boys' allergies might be caused by secondhand smoke.

I got out of the car. He threw the phone bill at me. The pages flew up, fell down.

'Get the fuck out of here.'

'Paul.'

'I'm taking the boys to San Salvador while you move out. Then I'm going to divorce you. Then I'm going to kill that greasy mother-fucker. Then I'll put him out of business. Then I'll destroy his reputation. He's not the only one with friends in this country. I know what kind of deals he's doing. 'Banking.' Banking my ass. He's a money launderer. He's a fucking vacuum cleaner.'

'Paul.'

'Do you realize he's borrowed on every one of his properties from half a dozen different banks? That's illegal, Brett. It's called pyramid financing. Do you even know where his money comes from?'

'I love you, Paul.'

'He's a fucking drug dealer. He's a glorified drug dealer. He cleans drug money for a living.'

'Paul, it's not what you think. I don't care about him. It's over. It means nothing.'

'Do you know how many women he fucks? Do you know how many women he's fucked in the past month? Do you know how many times he's tried to get me to go to a whorehouse?'

The fight continued inside. I was glad he let me in. The boys hid from us. It went on for more than two hours the same way. Paul planned to leave in the morning, but he agreed to let me spend the night. I went to sleep on the far side of my side of the bed, but I reached out with a foot to touch his leg. He let it rest there. I thought, This is a hopeful sign.

I woke to shouting. 'Look at this, you slut!'

'What?' The room was dark and I was still asleep.

'You whore!' He threw my cellphone, and it shattered on the wall. I climbed out of bed to get it but he beat me there.

'Just look.'

'Okay,' I reached out for the phone and he jerked it back. I said, 'What does it say?'

'Look at it! Don't try to take it!' He held it in his hand and showed me the screen.

There were four texts. They were between Paul and Eduard, who was listed in my phone as 'Supermart Pharmacy.'

Paul (to Supermart Pharmacy): What r u doin?

Supermart Pharmacy: Nothing. What are you doing?

Paul: Fighting with Paul.
Supermart Pharmacy: Oh, I'm sorry. Be
  kind to him.

I tried to take the phone from Paul. I wanted to text Eduard and tell him that he had been texting with Paul, not me. Paul went to the bathroom and dropped my phone into the toilet. He said, 'Get out.'

At three a.m. I checked into The Raphael. The desk clerk was carefully groomed, and she gave me and my torn jeans and thousand-dollar heels a look of sympathy and superiority. The hotel room was white, silent and uncluttered. It was a nice hotel room. I thought about the hotel room I'd stayed in the night I left my first husband, years before, in Dallas. I went to the bathroom and saw I'd left our house so quickly I hadn't rubbed my face cream in all the way. I had a very tiny smear above my cheekbone. I thought, Well, ready for round two.

PART TWO

PART TWO

1

'I want you to try on engagement rings,' Eduard said. 'Just for fun.'

We were in San Salvador. He'd found us a hotel with a beach we could walk on. We woke early and walked along the beach for more than an hour. We climbed a hill covered with vines and on the other side there was a sea cave. We took off our shoes and our clothes and put them on a high rock and swam naked. We were in the water for half an hour and Eduard said, 'Look!' and caught his own wallet floating in the water. He found my shoes in the surf. There was no beach left by our cave and we had to swim out beyond and around the rocks with our clothes in our hands to get back to land. I had wanted to make love on the sand in that cave.

I was hungry but I was hungry in that nice beach way, when you don't have to eat if you don't want to.

He rented a convertible. We'd never driven together in a convertible before and I turned the radio up loud. It was not hot in El Salvador that May. He told me that we should put the top up when we were on the highway but I didn't want to put it up. We never put the top up on that car once the whole week we were in San Salvador. It never rained.

'Well, this is the place,' he said. It was a narrow street but the sun came straight down into it. A dog walked up to our car and started to sniff it. The car was expensive enough that no one would mess with it, for fear of who might own it.

Everywhere you went in Central America, at this time, if you were in a town or a city, you saw serious young brown skinny men with large rifles and sub-machine guns. I expect it is still the same way today. Two of them stood on each corner of this street. One smoked a cigarette and watched us shyly.

We went into the jewelry store. It was hidden in a bank building, upstairs, and we walked through several anonymous offices and two locked doors before sitting down in a small wallpapered room. They brought us glasses of champagne. I drank mine without hesitating and asked for another. Eduard frowned.

We all sat at a small, elegant table. I'd taken off my wedding ring. 'She likes emerald cuts and cushion cuts,' Eduard explained to the jeweler. He was a chubby man with slicked-back gray hair in a black suit. He lay a diamond cloth open on the table.

'One carat? A carat and a half?' He had an Italian accent.

'Nothing under two,' Eduard said. 'She likes fancy colors, if you have a vivid yellow. She also likes pinks.'

'We don't have any pink diamonds over half a carat, Señor Carranza.'

My best friend from college wore a two-carat pink diamond for her wedding ring. She was an attorney in Mexico City, and she handled some business for us. Eduard had met her and he knew I admired her ring.

'I do have a lovely three-stone ring with quarter-carat pinks on either side. The center stone in a carat-and-a-half round, D Flawless. But of course I can call in a larger stone for you. I have the papers on several pinks from our partner store in Rio de Janeiro.'

I had a third glass of champagne. Eduard had a second. He looked at a dozen loose diamonds and chose a 2.45-carat cushion cut, F VVS1, $88,500. The jeweler placed it on the back of my closed fingers and said, 'Wear it out into the sunlight.' The security guard started to walk out with us but the salesman brushed him back into the store.

We stood in the sunlight and looked at the diamond. I said, 'It's not what I had in mind.'

'It's beautiful,' Eduard said. He put his

hand on my back.

'I'm not sure.'

We were playing.

The salesman said, 'She wants a pink. She's right.' He gave Eduard his card.

'If I can call you, sir, I'll arrange several pinks to show you and the lady.' He bent toward me with a smile. 'I can have them here by Wednesday.'

'I'll call you,' Eduard said. He took the stone off my fingers, looked at me for a moment, and returned it to the man, who took it from him with the diamond cloth and cleaned it before tucking it in his breast pocket. He went back inside after shaking hands. Eduard put his arm around my waist. 'Thank you,' he said. 'That was fun.'

2

We went to a local place he knew near the cathedral and got drunk on the owner's private collection of Peruvian brandy. I decided to drink as much as I wanted. I wanted to celebrate.

I looked at Eduard. I said, 'I'm free. You don't know how good it feels.'

'Are you hungry?' Eduard said.

'No. Are you?'

'I'll order a few things. The food's good here.'

When I went to the bathroom I looked in the mirror. My face looked strange. Careful, Brett, I thought. I splashed my face with water, and I went back to the table. I noticed the waiter seemed nervous. I ordered another round, and I thought, That waiter's afraid of me.

'That jeweler liked your chain,' I said to Eduard. I had given him a heavy 18-carat gold Bulgari chain when we were in Miami. It was the only piece of jewelry I'd ever given a man.

'He was too busy checking out your cleavage,' he said.

I took a big swallow of my drink. It was

already empty. I took a sip of Eduard's and waved to the waiter. 'Do you take that necklace off?'

'I never take it off. You know that.'

'I mean, when you're fucking Lurisia.'

He frowned.

'Does it slap her tits?'

'What?'

'You heard me. Does your necklace slap Lurisia's tits, when you fuck her? Or anybody. When you fuck your whores.'

I finished his brandy. The waiter came to the table and I ordered two more.

'Can you make a pisco sour?' I asked him. 'Two pisco sours.'

'Just one, for the lady,' Eduard said. 'Brett, what's up? A minute ago we were having a perfectly pleasant conversation. I think you should eat.'

'Do they grab it? Your whores. When you eat them out.'

'For Chrissake, Brett.'

'I just want to hear about your necklace, Eduard. The one I gave you. Do they wrap it around your cock?'

He stood up from the table. 'Brett, I don't know what's come over you. But the way you're talking to me is not — '

'Is not what? Now that I'm finally telling the truth. Is not what, Eduard? Tell me. Tell me the truth for once.'

'Come with me, Brett. Let's get something to eat in the room.'

'I'm staying right where I am. You go, then. Get out of here.'

'I'm going back to the hotel.'

'I guess it just lays between their tits,' I said. 'The chain I mean. Unless you're about to come. Then it probably slaps them.' The waiter brought me a pisco sour. I said, 'You switch it around backwards, between your shoulder blades, the same way you do when you fuck me.'

'Goodnight, Brett.'

'I'll let you know when I make up my mind. Go to sleep. If I want to I'll wake you up.'

'We can talk in the morning.'

3

It was the first time Eduard had seen me in a blackout. He told me about it the next day. I didn't quite believe him. I told him I was sorry. But still it was strange because it seemed to me like we'd only been at the bar for half an hour.

'Listen, I know you don't want to hear this right now, but I have to have a drink.'

'Let's have mimosas. Room service.'

4

Paul had stayed with his parents for two weeks and now he and his sons were back in the house. I had promised Paul that I would be moved out, but I had not packed any more than the first suitcase. I hadn't even gone home. I had been living at The Raphael and going on vacation with Eduard. I had been shopping. I drank when I shopped. I had begun to dress differently, in expensive clothes. I was popular with the salespeople. I wrote a story about a man who kills a Mexican prostitute. Then I wrote one about an effeminate old man who falls in love with a twenty-year-old. I sent them to my agent and she placed them immediately. She wrote, 'Whatever it is you're doing, don't stop.'

I had also promised Paul that I wouldn't see Eduard. Eduard had told Paul that his relationship with me had been a fling and Paul believed him, though he insisted that one of Eduard's partners take over our business banking. I knew the most important thing I could do was stay in touch with Paul, but I couldn't make myself call him. I didn't want to lie to him.

But Eduard was always trying to make me call him. 'If he doesn't hear from you, he'll think we're together,' he said. 'How hard is it to lie, Brett? How many lies have you told Paul in your life? How many has he told you?'

'He doesn't really lie.'

'You think he tells you the truth about everything?'

'This is different. I can't lie to him. I can't just say you're not here. Just lie about everything that's going on. I'm not like you, Eduard. You're like a master thief who sees a kid stealing candy and says, 'See, everybody lies.' Most people don't really lie that much. It doesn't come naturally.'

Eduard could lie to Lurisia — they still lived together — to his clients, his boss, to me, to friends, all of them, effortlessly. I'd seen him do it. He said that like most highly intelligent people, he was a liar.

'I'd rather tell him the truth. I'd rather everybody just know the truth,' I said. 'Why do you care what I do, or who I tell? You don't tell anyone. You hide me like a secret. You're ashamed of me.'

'What possible difference could it make to Paul whether what you're telling him is true of false? One difference. Whether or not you're hurting him. Hurting him and us.'

I wanted Eduard to be proud of me. I

wanted him to reveal the truth about us. I wanted Eduard to tell Lurisia, his parents and his friends: I'm in love with Brett. But you can't make your lover do that. Once I worked at a magazine and the publisher sent around a folded memo that read: 'I demand respect!' Same situation here. You can't make your lover love you. At least not by direct means.

'Fine. You win. I'll call him.'

Bella answered. Bella hated me now. 'That Brett,' she said, 'is on the phone.' She gave the phone to Paul, and I lied to him for twenty minutes. I told him I wasn't moved out yet, I had been with my mother — she was sick. I could hear him hearing the lies. He understood: I was in love with a Mexican banker.

5

On a flight back to Mexico City from visiting
Eduard in Panama I upgraded myself to first
class at check-in. Waiting for the plane, I had
three double margaritas. They seemed like
light pours to me, but when I sat down I
remember feeling a bit odd. A middle-aged
woman sitting across the aisle from me
frowned when I ordered a drink before the
plane took off. She was probably about my
age but she was dressed in St. John. The flight
attendant brought me a bottle of red wine
and I held it in my lap.

I tried to be friendly with the woman
across the aisle, but I could hear myself
slurring my words. I was probably repeating
myself. The next thing I remember distinctly
was when she said, 'Would you please watch
your language.'

She took an embroidering kit out of her
bag and started to needlepoint. 'I like the
pattern,' I said.

She ignored me.

'Have you been sewing for long? That's
quite a hobby.' I poured myself a glass of wine
and drank it. The bottle was full so the flight

attendant must have brought me another.

'Is that for your mom? Or for a friend?' She kept on sewing.

'My maid sews. I mean, that's not an insult. My grandmother sewed. She did embroidery.'

The woman ignored me.

'It used to be a sign of effluence. Aff — affluence. It is still, having the leisure to needlepoint.'

The woman put her work down and turned to face me. She said very distinctly, 'Can you stop talking?'

I reached up an arm and pushed the flight attendant call button. When the flight attendant came, I said, 'This woman beside me just threatened to stab me with that needle.'

'I'm sorry, ma'am?'

'The woman tried to stab me. Said she was going to take the plane down.'

The needlepoint woman protested.

'Ma'am, is there a problem here?'

'She pointed her needle at me. She said she was going to jab me. The needle needs to go. Or she needs to go in back. I mean, one or the other. You pick. She's crazy.'

'I don't know what she's talking about.' The woman seemed nervous.

'You know, you know. You can't fool these

95

people. They're experts.'

'Ma'am, I think you should calm down.'

'I am not safe in this seat. I think she should put that needle away or be taken off the plane. I mean, if you need to land this thing, I understand.' I gave the woman with the needle a look like, See what you just did? No more first class for you, lady.

The flight attendant was looking at my wine. She left. Then a man in a blue shirt and khakis appeared.

'Ma'am, I'm the air marshal on this flight.'

'Finally.'

'Ma'am, I'll need you to come with me.'

I didn't know where to put my wine bottle. The latch on the seat-tray beside me wasn't working. Then my tray wouldn't latch up.

'I'll handle that for you, ma'am,' the marshal said, and took my bottle of wine.

I followed him up to the galley.

'Ma'am, I want you to understand this is serious.'

'I unnerstand.'

'The accusations you have made are serious. You do understand that.'

'Yes, sir.'

'Tell me again. What happened?'

'Yes, officer.'

'Tell me.'

'Yes, sir.'

'Ma'am, you're not answering my question. I'm asking you to tell me what happened between you and the other passenger.'

'The needle. She's got a needle.'

'Okay.'

'She said she was going to take the plane down.'

'You're positive? You don't think you might have misunderstood her, or . . . anything like that?'

'No, sir.'

'The passenger next to you in seat 3C told you that she was going to take the plane down with her sewing needle. That's what happened?'

'As far as I can tell.'

'Ok ma'am. This is what happens next. So that you are very clear. We are going to have to land the plane. I am going to have to call the Mexican police. They will take each of you to interrogation rooms, and you will both be questioned.'

'Do you think she may have been kidding?'

'Well, I wasn't there. I am asking you.'

'She looks harmless. She looks like my grandmother.'

'Well ma'am, the charges you made are serious, but I can see you've been drinking, and so I'm just going to put you in the back of the plane. But I want you to know this is not a game. You're on an international flight.'

'I'm sorry if I caused any confusion. You know, she's just sewing. My grandmother does it too. She's just sewing. A person should be allowed to sew. On a plane.'

'Let's get you back to your seat.'

'You can't sew without a needle. She's just. You know. Needlepoint.'

'Yes, ma'am.'

They moved me out of first class, to the back of the plane. I didn't protest. I tried to order a whiskey but the flight attendant in economy told me they were out of whiskey. 'A vodka? A beer?' He ignored me.

6

When we landed I was almost sober. I called Eduard from the taxi to The Raphael. 'I almost got myself arrested.'

I told the story, and I was surprised that Eduard laughed the whole way through.

'You got what was coming to you. She won. She had old lady magic. Besides, it sounds like you were hammered.'

He was in his and Lurisia's apartment. I was getting nearer asking him when he planned to move out. One of you has to move out first, I reminded myself. I was the one to move out first when I left my first husband, too.

'What's old lady magic?' I said.

'How they cut in lines, all that.'

'She wasn't even old! She was my age. And I wasn't that drunk. I wasn't even drunk enough for anyone to notice.'

'Obviously not,' Eduard said. But he was laughing with me, and it was nice, to laugh with someone about one of my drunk stories. I'd missed that when I was sober.

7

A month, perhaps two months went by. I started asking to come back home. Paul's family wanted a divorce, the quicker the better. His therapist said that he deserved better.

'People have affairs, Paul. It doesn't mean the marriage ends. It means we have problems. I'm sorry. I did a horrible thing. But I love you. I love our sons. I want to come home.'

'It's too much. I can't do it any more.'

'The first time we are really on the rocks you just divorce me?'

'It's not the first time, Brett. I put up with your drinking for six years. You tried to kill yourself with my son five feet away from you.' He had never called him, 'my son.' He made a point of saying, 'our sons,' and even, 'your sons.' The suicide attempt was from my novel.

It had happened, but not the way I told it in the book. He was quoting my own fiction back at me.

'You know as well as I do that suicide attempt was ridiculous. I was hanging myself with a sheet, Paul. Our son was asleep. I was trying to get your attention. I was trying to tell you that I'd been secretly drinking for three years without having to face the consequences.'

'That's my point. Three years of lying. Not to mention all the other lies. It's not worth it. I can never trust you again. You're a sociopath.' When in years past friends of ours had joked with him about my lies and exaggerations, Paul had always said, 'Brett is the most honest person I've ever met.' He wasn't joking. He thought I didn't tell the fake social lies that everybody else did. He knew I never pretended to be someone other than who I was. He also genuinely believed that he was the one person I would never lie to.

8

Paul and I met in a film class on Almodovar at the University of Texas at Austin shortly after I left my first husband. During seminar breaks I pretended to smoke so that there was a reason to hang out with him. After seminar one afternoon we went with a friend of his to have beers and play pool at The Showdown on Guadalupe. It's a bar that people who know Austin know about. He was skinny, his blond hair brushed his shoulders then. He had small wrists and narrow shoulders, and I liked the way he dressed. He wore these worn-out tweed coats — all wrong for the weather, but right on him, and he had a clumsy way of bending over the pool table that I liked. He liked to drink. Everyone who met him immediately told him, if the opportunity presented itself, that he had astonishing eyes. They are enormous, and a color of blue I have not seen anywhere else. Unlike most everyone's eyes, they are almost always the same color.

9

He was in the film studies grad student study lounge on the third floor of Ryan Hall in a collared windowpane shirt, green crewneck sweater and grey wool slacks. He sat on the sofa with his legs crossed, like a girl, I thought. Later he told me that actually it is a woman who should cross her legs at the ankle, and a man at the knee. He was talking to one of the famous visiting professors. I came into the office and sat down on the other side of the sofa.

'I'm hungry,' I said. 'Are you hungry? Do you want to get some lunch?'

10

We sat outside at The Shady Grove. We both had Bloody Marys. I think we had four each. I had a plate of vegetables with a smoked green chili sauce — I was a vegetarian at this time, and had dropped to one hundred and five pounds — and he had a fried chicken sandwich with gravy, which is the best thing there. I had to drive drunk to my seminar.

In the next few days I disentangled myself from relationships with three other men I was dating at this time. After one date with Paul I knew I didn't want to see other men. Then he asked me out.

When he picked me up for dinner I was in a short green dress. I was wearing too much eye make-up. I noticed he had bought new pants and a new jacket for the date. He didn't know that was one of my favorite things about him — nothing he wore was new.

At the restaurant, walking in, I called him 'Sam.' Sam was a man I had been dating. Paul missed a step and then continued walking as though he hadn't noticed. Inside I apologized, and explained that I wasn't seeing Sam anymore.

After we opened our menus and he chose a bottle of wine I said, 'Let's eat a lot of food.'

For years afterward he repeated that remark back to me, as the first time he knew that he might fall in love with me.

After dinner, Paul came back to my apartment and we sat on the sofa together. It was an enormous sofa. It came with the apartment and looked like it had been made in the late seventies with burlap bags. I'd bought two blankets at Urban Outfitters to try to make it presentable but it didn't quite work.

I was apologizing for the sofa. I was apologizing for the whole apartment. 'Would it be alright if kissed you?' he asked. We kissed on the sofa and he kissed like a hungry tiger might make out with you.

'Hey, slow down,' I said after a minute. 'There's no rush.'

'Are you making fun of the way I kiss?'

'No. You're a great kisser. I just — there's no hurry. We can kiss all night.'

He changed his kiss then and we kissed more gently, calmly, and deeply. I was reassured because I saw we would be able to kiss together after all.

If you can't kiss each other, there's no point in continuing.

Eventually we moved to the bed, and he

had my hand between my legs, and then his face between my legs, but I wouldn't let him take down my leggings. I was squirming.

'This is ridiculous,' he said at last. 'You're obviously as frustrated as I am. Let's have sex.'

'No,' I said, and pushed him away. 'We can kiss if you want. But we're not having sex. I don't know you well enough yet.'

'You know me. Don't lie. Look at me.' He kissed me again, and we kept our eyes open. I squeezed his hips between my legs. 'Tell me you don't want me to fuck you.'

'No!' I said. I laughed and wriggled away. We wrestled.

'Okay, okay,' he said. 'Let's have a glass of wine.'

Months later, Paul asked me, 'Why didn't you sleep with me that night?'

11

Cheating on your husband is a lot like doing cocaine. It's rarely pleasurable, but try quitting.

Eduard left Lurisia and moved into a new place. At night in his condo we often sat on his balcony and listened to Bob Dylan and watched the people in the streets below. We'd take pillows from the bed, I'd be between his legs with his arms around me and I'd turn my head so that we could kiss.

'Next summer we'll get some of those misting things for out here,' I said. 'That way we can come out all summer long. We could sleep out here. With a big mosquito net.'

'Good idea,' he said, and the way he said it, like we would never make it to next summer, made us both quiet for a few minutes.

'Does Paul want you back?' he asked.

'That's the worst part,' I lied. 'He wants it so much. But I can't go back. I'm in love with you. A week would go by and I would be on a plane to you again.'

That part was true.

12

I didn't drink when I was alone in Mexico City, mostly, but I was always drinking when I was with Eduard. I always drank on the way to see him, and sometimes on the way back.

He didn't like to drink with me, now, so I'd drink when he wasn't around.

One night, coming back from a trip Eduard and I took to Peru, I had a blackout. I remember buying margaritas for everyone at the airport bar. Eduard and I had taken separate flights home. I was on a layover and I didn't know what airport I was in. I woke up in the hospital in Mexico City. I had cracked my head on the stone stairs outside the hotel. Eduard said I had called him late that night. 'You said you'd been arrested, and then they let you go.'

The next day, Paul came to get me at the hospital.

'You're not stable. You have to get sober, Brett. You can't live in a hotel.'

I was picking at the staples in my hair with my fingers.

'I want to spend time with the boys,' I said. 'I miss them so much. You don't know how much I love them. Even if you're not going to talk to me, I have to see the boys.'

He had been dating friends of ours in Mexico City — he'd even been sleeping around — but I knew he hadn't fallen in love. His parents were spending a lot of time in town. Sadie kept trying to talk me into moving in with her in Galveston.

'The boys miss you,' Paul said. 'How about we make a deal. You go back to Minnesota and dry out. You loved it there. Go to Hazelden and I'll think about things.'

'I was miserable.'

'It worked, Brett. If you'll spend thirty days there, you can see the boys once a week. Or every other weekend, even, if you get an apartment. They can't spend the night with you at a hotel.'

13

I'd go seven days, ten days, two days sober. Then in Puerto Vallarta or some other city I'd take a drink. By this time, I hid it from everybody — even Eduard thought I'd quit.

I was back to my old tricks.

When a normal person walks into a restaurant she looks for the best table, the most cheerful location, a sunny spot or an intimate corner. Or she doesn't think much about it at all: she lets the hostess or her date decide. A secret drinker maps the restaurant like a bank robber maps a score. She locates the bar, the women's room, and the (usually small) group of tables that allow her to pass the bar while on her way to the bathroom without her date being able to see her. Supporting pillars are good; ideally, she wants a blind spot where he cannot spot her even if he turns his head. A man will watch his woman as she comes and goes in a way that a woman will not watch her man, not because he is suspicious of her, but because he likes to watch her move. The secret drinker looks for restaurants with bars next door: if necessary, she can exit out the back, take a quick drink at the neighboring place, and come back again. On his first drink the secret drinker will tip the bartender at least as much as the cost of the drink, so she's made a friend. The secret drinker will wait outside the bathroom, motion to her waiter, ask him to bring a drink — 'a double vodka, I'll just drink it right here, and pay for it now' — if there is no way to approach the bar, or no bar in the restaurant. She will casually flirt with the bartender or the waiter to try to make him part of the game. The secret drinker can open a bottle of beer with any hard object: the edge of the lock in the bathroom stall, a counter top, the nut on a pipe, a key in her pocket, in desperation her thumbnail. The secret drinker always carries cash with her. She cleans out half the bottles in the minibar and refills them with water while her lover is shaving. She is quick to pour her lover a drink if he wants one — though the bottles she's drunk will be in the back of the refrigerator, where he is unlikely to take one. Above all, the secret drinker keeps her lover drunk. Because a sober lover can tell if you've been drinking. He keeps track of time and how often you've been to the bathroom. He notices you've been gone to the convenience store for half an hour when it should have taken ten minutes. With a drunk lover you can drink all night long.

14

At times when I was very drunk Eduard would record what I had said the night before. 'No post-mortems' had been a rule, but we were past that. It started when he went to the bathroom and saw I had peed on the floor. He mentioned it to me when he got back into bed — he woke me up to tell me. And he turned on his phone so that I would have to hear it.

'I doan see what the big deal is.'

'Brett. You were too drunk to find the toilet.'

'Did you fuck me while I was passed out?'

'Let's go back to sleep.'

'Did we have sex? Is your come inside me?'

'Brett. Can you hear yourself?'

'How many times did you fuck me when I was out?'

'I can't believe the things you're saying.'

'For me, Eduard, sex and emotion are all bound up together. Most of the — 95 percent of the sexual experience I had, was when I was — you know what? You were right before, we're not right for each other. I'm not right for you.'

Silence.

'It's fine. Really, it's all fine. It's lucky we found out when we did. I'm just glad we're finally telling the truth.'

'Brett, go to sleep. Everything is alright.'

'Yup. You did. It's for the best. I'm just glad we finally got it out into the open.'

'Brett, I never said that.'

'You don't love me. You just took the first woman who came along. You bastard.'

'Shh.'

'No matter how hard I try, it's never good enough for you. Nobody can say — nobody can say I didn't try.'

'Brett.'

'Don't say, 'Brett.' You're ashamed of me. When I'm the one who should be ashamed.'

'I'm going. I'm going to get a different room in the hotel.'

'Everyone knows about your sluts. Your whores. Paul told me. He's told everyone. It's like a joke. All your friends know. A man can be a slut too. Look at yourself in the mirror.'

Insights of this kind by the blacked-out me.

15

I told him I had a secret fortune that I would be awarded by my dead grandparents when I turned forty. 'Hundreds of millions, neither one of us will ever work again.' I told him about imaginary stories and novels I had written or published. I told him about famous men in pursuit of me, men I spurned for his sake. I promised suicide.

It is hard, even for a practiced drunk, to take responsibility for things she says or does during a blackout. When you have no recollection of doing something, it's as though it's been done by an evil stranger who hates you, and who has decided to possess your body in order to destroy everything that you love. As a way of murdering you.

'You're like Dr. Jekyll and Mr. Hyde,' Eduard said.

'I've never heard that one before.'

'This isn't a joke. Why won't you just admit it when you're drunk? You need professional help, Brett.'

'I'm not drunk half as often as you think I am.'

'If that's true, you're in even worse shape

than I thought. Alcoholism I can understand. This other person you become, when you're in one of your fugues' — that's what he called my drunk moods, when I was at my worst — 'is dangerous. You don't know what you're doing. You could get hurt, Brett. You could be raped. There's no telling what could happen.'

'My psychiatrist says I'm fine as long as I stay sober. And I'm telling you, I've quit drinking. Give me a chance. Let's go to Cancun, where we first met. We'll spend a few days there and then drive down the coast. I'll show you. Anyway, I want to see that new place in Valladolid. Those people are making a name for themselves.'

'What place? I don't know about it.'

'Some couple Paul told me about. He says they're knocking him off. It will be fun to look. We'll be like spies.'

I don't know what might have happened next if Eduard hadn't agreed.

16

In Cancun I knew I was going to stay sober. Since Paul had tossed me out I realized how much I needed to see my boys. I wanted Eduard to believe in us. I didn't want to wake up to the forensics of ghastly fights I didn't even remember.

His flight came in to Mexico City and I bought him a whiskey at the bar.

'I don't have to drink,' he said. 'Honestly, I don't want to.'

'It won't work that way,' I said. 'I have to be sober for myself. And if you stop drinking just for me you'll resent me. Or you'll only drink when we're not together and you'll want a drink when we are. Or you'll have more fun when you're drinking with your friends and I'll seem dull because you never get to have a drink.' This last certainty was the one I feared the most.

'I don't think any of those statements are correct. I'm happy to stop drinking. It's not that big of a deal for me.'

'It isn't now,' I said. 'But that's because you're free to drink. If you feel like you can't,

117

it's going to come between us. Just trust me on this one.'

'Did it come between you and Paul?'

He had me there. Once I was properly sober, the time Paul and I had together when we weren't drinking was perhaps the best time of our marriage.

'Am I with Paul now? And what's the first thing he did when we split up? Started drinking again.'

It was true. Paul was drinking with his dad. I spent hours lying in bed in my hotel room, imagining the things they were saying about me. Or that, worst still, they were drunk together and I never came up.

'Fine, fine, I'll drink the whiskey. Hell, I could use it. You look great. I've got to go to the bathroom, I'll be right back.'

I knew he was lying about how I looked. And I knew he was texting Lurisia in the men's room.

17

The hotel in Cancun was new and extravagant, but too big. Eduard knew the owner and I was relieved when he told me that we didn't have to go out with him. We were on the beach. The room was made of blue marble — Italian rather than Mexican — pale yellow silk, and glass.

'Let's change hotels,' I said.

'This is the best hotel in Cancun. They just built the damn thing. It's gorgeous.'

'It's great,' I said. 'Thank you. But I don't feel like we're safe here. Do you know what I mean? Let's find a little place. I don't even care if we're on the beach. I want to feel like I have you all to myself.'

'You're crazy,' he said. 'Whatever Brett wants, Brett gets.' He made love to me on the bed, and then he got on the phone while I took a bath and found us a different place.

18

It was one of those vacation places where no one minds if a couple is falling all over each other. Our new hotel room had windows on three walls. One was above the bed, and another overlooked a stairwell. Through both windows we could see palm fronds and bougainvillea in pink, red and orange, and many other tropical flowers I didn't know. We could hear the birds screaming in the trees and smell the sea. I hadn't been drinking for almost a week now and my sex drive was back. I insisted that we keep the windows open and the curtains back when we had sex. We were noisy in bed.

'At least let me shut them,' he said. 'If I can't pull the curtains.'

Eduard had my arms behind my back, my legs between his, and he was fucking me as hard as he could from behind while I groaned. I saw a man who looked Cuban position himself behind a post on the stairs. He was five feet from our bed. He peered around the post every few seconds and caught my eye. He smiled at me.

'I can never predict what you're going to be

prudish about,' I said, after we finished.

'I'm Catholic. I'm shy,' he said, smiling. 'Plus, I mean this is not exactly prudish. We are being exhibitionists.'

'I don't see what there is to be ashamed of.'

But I couldn't hide my expression and he knew I enjoyed it.

19

Our hotel didn't have a pool, and later we went to the pool at a property Madonna owned or had owned and I ordered Eduard a drink so that we had a right to swim. A couple who had rented a cabana told us we could lay in their deck chairs. I was tan all this year — it was almost exactly a year, now, since Eduard and I had started — but I needed some sun on my skin. My upper lip had broken out in tiny pimples like a moustache. Eduard drank his mojito, I drank my Coke Light. I did not want a drink. We watched the fat burned white people and ripped Asian boys and skinny haughty boys in sunglasses. One girl with shoulder-length glossy black hair that hadn't been wet yet stared at Eduard through her aviators. She was standing in the water at the end of the pool with the sun showing on her tight body. Her swimsuit was expensive, red with an orange stripe, and snug. She was drinking cognac from a snifter.

'Do you want to get in the water?' Eduard asked.

'Sure.'

I watched him perform in the pool for this young woman. He went underwater and tossed his head back when he came to the surface. He swam laps then stretched his arms and back. He did a backflip off the diving board. I might have done something similar if a beautiful young man were admiring me. Still I was irritated. I stood on a small fountain in the middle of the pool. I was out of the water to about my knees, and I saw that, in the white bikini shorts I had bought, you could see everything.

'Honey,' Eduard said. 'Come back into the pool. Let me hold you in the water.'

'I will,' I said. I thought, How do you like it?

He swam to the side and put his sunglasses on. Everyone looks ridiculous when they wear their sunglasses in a swimming pool. But Eduard was wearing his sunglasses in Madonna's swimming pool.

'Maybe we should have bought black shorts for you,' Eduard said. He swam back out toward me. 'Or colored ones. The white ones are a little transparent now that they're wet.'

I glanced down. 'They're fine. You are so paranoid. Besides, you're the one who's showing off.'

'Hey, I'm missing you down here,' Eduard said. Miss Asian Perfect Body was still watching him. Other people had noticed me. I saw women talking quietly to each other and motioning with their chins the way they do.

I got back into the water. Eduard carried me around the pool.

'You're being silly,' I said.

I went and got his mojito from our pool table. Now most of the people there noticed my transparent shorts.

'Pool drinks,' I said when I got back to Eduard. It was a joke that Paul used to make.

When we got out of the pool, the couple had taken their deck chairs back.

'Sorry,' the man said. The woman regarded me without an expression. Eduard wrapped me in a towel, then put one around himself.

The beautiful young Asian woman hadn't moved from her spot. But now she was eyeing someone else's man.

She'll learn, I thought.

Then I thought, No. As long as there's a market for it, people will always be looking at each other, and enjoying being watched. In the god realm, the Mayans said, they make love by exchanging glances.

Paul's mother told me once, 'The worst thing about growing old is that you become invisible.' Only a beautiful woman could know something that awful.

20

I said, 'I want to take you out tonight. You're always paying. Let me buy tonight.'

'You could buy drinks before dinner. How about that?'

'You choose a place.'

He chose the Ritz, which was a good sign. We had made love very gently and for a long time before we went out, and we were happy. We walked along the edge of the sea in the dark. He carried my heels and we held hands. There was no moon, and the water was quiet. From the beach the Ritz-Carleton looked like the nicest hotel in Cancun, but the bar was empty except for three discouraged middle-aged women. They looked like businesspeople or corporate saleswomen of some kind, but there is no business in Cancun.

The pools of the hotel were illuminated and the lights shone across the bar and gave the air an underwater feeling. The women could have been holding their breath, or their gills might have opened, or they could be drowned, I thought. They looked at Eduard with frank appreciation.

It is exhausting dating a sexual man. Every

time you walk into a bar or restaurant there they are, all the predators who want to take him from you.

'I want a whiskey,' Eduard told the bartender. 'With just one cube of ice. She'll have a Coke Light.'

The bartender poured him four fingers of whiskey in the glass. I saw him look at the bartender — she was a tiny thing, my size or smaller, she couldn't have weighed ninety pounds — and she moved on down the bar.

It was one of those half-inside-half-outside bars they have at resorts in the tropics.

Eduard took two long sips of his whiskey. He was wearing a linen suit that he knew I loved. I wiped off my lipstick with a cocktail napkin and kissed him.

'I love you,' he said. 'I really want us to be together.'

They were playing old American country music. Eduard finished his drink in three big swallows and ordered another. The bartender poured it the same. He drank it down, and ordered a third.

'What's gotten into you?'

'Let's get in the pool. Come into the pool with me,' he said. He got a fourth to carry with him.

'I'll watch you.'

'You're no fun,' he said.

He took off his shoes, rolled up his trousers to the knee, and walked between the bar pool and the larger infinity pool. The two pools were connected by a shallow underwater ledge. Walking along it, the water reached Eduard's calves. He took his pants off. He wore yellow silk boxers with elephants printed on them. Both pools were illuminated and the blue light shone up on him from below. He took his shirt off and dipped in the water. The women had perked up. I took pictures with my phone. Eduard took his underwear off, and threw it towards me in a ball. They landed in the pool and floated conspicuously. A husband had arrived and he gave me a questioning look. Even the bartender raised his eyebrows at me.

Eduard was singing in Spanish, in his strong soprano, with his penis flapping around, but he wasn't slurring his words. It was a love song he was singing to the night.

I picked up my Coke Light and moved to a table closer to the pool. It had been raining earlier and I brushed off the cushions before sitting. The cushion soaked the ass of my dress.

'Come on, come out here!' Eduard shouted. I smiled and waved. Just a week ago this would have been the time to drink half of his whiskey, I thought. But I didn't want it.

It may have been stubbornness. No alcoholic, no matter how practiced, whether she's had twenty relapses or never had one in twenty years, can explain why she doesn't take a drink.

He was dancing a tango with himself. I didn't know what I would do if he fell the wrong way. Presumably one of the hotel staff would rescue him. I'd never seen him truly drunk before. He seemed larger. At last he came back to sit with me. He put his clothes back on carefully. He looked around for his underwear, which had at last sunk into the pool. Without getting up, I looked around for his shoes. He walked around barefoot. Then he sat, and quickly stood up again. He wobbled, held the arms of the chair, and sat back down.

'This chair. Got my pants wet.' He took a sip of his whiskey. 'Did you like my song?'

I showed him the pictures. He laughed. He looked handsome. Drunk and bold and blue in the pool lights and silly. I showed them to him again the next day, performing a post-mortem of my own, and he still loved them.

'Hey, Julio Iglesias,' I said, 'who's the exhibitionist now?' And he laughed and said, 'What's good for the goose.'

We borrowed a convertible from the

Mercedes dealer in town — he was a friend of Eduard's — and drove to a house at the end of the peninsula. That night there was a storm and when we woke the ocean and the seaside had been swept clean. The house was down on the sand, and the glass doors of our bedroom opened to the beach and the sea not even fifty yards away.

'Let's get in the ocean,' he said.

'Okay, in a minute.' No one was up yet. Further down people lived on the beach in little straw huts, and cooked fish, rice and plantains. You could walk across a channel into the grassy jungles of Belize.

Before Cancun, I had told him that everything would be alright with me, again, if I could swim in the ocean with him and see the sun on his skin. When I was sober, this seemed both impossible and true. If I had three drinks I saw it wasn't a dream at all, it was simply going to happen that way, it would all work out, if we were patient, if we could both be kind.

21

When we swam the water was too salty and we didn't stay out long. 'You're supposed to dive into the waves,' he told me.

'I know. I like to swim over them.'

When I was a kid in Florida my mom said she liked to watch me go into the surf. I clenched my fists like I wanted to conquer the ocean. I still prefer to stand in the waves and try to jump over them.

The way Eduard swam it was like he was trying to go somewhere.

Like a surfer swims in the ocean, but he wasn't headed for a break.

He held me in his arms, rolling up and down with the forming waves, cradling me and trying to get me to laugh, but it was like we were doing it because we had agreed we would, and it didn't work.

22

We never took a boat down to Honduras like we'd planned. We were happy where we were. I did not drink that whole week. But I drank alone, on the flight back to Mexico City. I drank five of those little bottles of wine. The flight attendants are only supposed to give you three, but I charmed mine. When I got off the plane I was elated. I had difficulty with my carry-on bag. In the cab, on the way to my new room at Suenos Realizados, I played Notorious B.I.G. on my iPhone, and discussed the racist lyrics with my driver, who was Jamaican and, for some reason, did not seem to mind. In fact, he liked me.

23

Sadie told me a story. She was just out of residency, and she had divorced her first husband. Her guru — Sadie's a Buddhist — was coming to Galveston. He wanted to see her, but she did not want to see him. She did not want to see him because, as she said, she was 'tired of feeling strange.' She wanted to just be a normal person, whatever that is. Her friends thought having a guru was corny. Sadie wanted to be like every other Texan psychiatrist, and to go to the depression conference in Dallas that coincided with her guru's visit, so that she would have a good excuse to avoid him.

The Buddhist community in Galveston — there is such a thing — was stirred up about it. People were driving down from Houston and Austin to see him speak.

She was ultimately persuaded to stay for her guru. He was staying with a wealthy host in Galveston and the household was being taken care of by several beautiful women from Tyler, Texas. The women of Tyler are as beautiful as one imagines the women from Texas are intended to be.

She was taken to see him in his room. She said for most of her life when she saw her guru, she rarely said anything. On this occasion, she started to cry, because she was divorced, bulimic, and her life seemed chaotic. Also, and more to the point, she cried because she thought she was ugly.

Her guru was quiet for a long time, and then he asked her why she was crying. She was too upset to answer, and she just cried more.

He said, 'Do you have a boyfriend?' She shook her head.

'Why don't you have a boyfriend?' he asked.

It occurred to her then that she had been divorced for almost three years.

He said, 'Is it because you are sad? They want a happy girlfriend.'

She said that she was happy when he told her this, because she knew that it was true.

When I left my first husband for another man, it was only because my husband was sad, and the new man was happy. Every time I walked into the room he lit up. The reason your marriage ends can be that simple.

24

The year was coming to an end.

'Where should we go for New Year's?'

'Nicaragua,' I said. Paul had taken me there before we were married. I wanted to see what it would look like, now, with my new eyes. And if it looks the same, I thought, maybe I'm meant to be back with Paul.

In Leon we stayed at a perfumerie with only one guest room. The high ceilings had beams, there was a chandelier over the freestanding tub and another chandelier over the four-poster bed, and the sun porch looked down on the little main street of the town. There was not much to do and we had too much time to talk. Whenever we knew we should be talking we had sex.

We were downstairs having coffee. The woman who ran the perfumerie made the coffee and Eduard invited her to sit with us. She was an American who had fallen in love with a local boy and now they were having a baby.

'The owners wanted to invite you to their home for New Year's Eve,' she said. 'It's their other hotel, at the ruins. It will be a nice group.'

The owners were both former models, an Argentinian and an Italian.

I didn't want to go but I knew that Eduard did, so I agreed.

'Did you see how disappointed she was?' I asked Eduard. 'She wanted to be invited to the dinner party.'

'I don't think so. I think she wanted to stay in town and watch the fireworks with her family,' Eduard said.

'Maybe so.'

It was funny, I thought, that his account of what the manager wanted to do was just what I wanted to do, and vice versa. I don't know which one of us was right. But it was characteristic of us that we assigned to other people the motivations and desires we suspected in each other.

25

The hotel by the ruins, where the models lived, was an hour from Leon. We found it as the sun was setting. It was next to a small lake but there were no mosquitoes because it was winter. A bonfire was burning and you could hear the occasional splash of a crocodile in the lake. The table was set for twelve.

We met the host and his wife.

'Eduard,' she said. 'I'm so glad you came. My husband told me about you two.'

Her husband was often in and out of the perfumerie. We had seen him several times, sometimes with a very beautiful Czech model who was clearly strung out on heroin. I could see the husband and the junkie were having an affair. The shockingly beautiful junkie was at the dinner with her boyfriend, a musician. But she could barely hold her head up.

'I'm sorry,' the host's wife said to me. She was sitting next to Eduard and her face was a bit too close. She had a lovely Italian accent and had recently had a baby. I was intimidated, and she was watching me carefully.

The host's wife said to me, 'I think I don't remember your name?'

'Her name is Brett.' Eduard jerked forward. 'It's strange. It's a boy's name.'

The hostess leaned across Eduard and shook my hand. 'Happy New Year,' she said.

26

Through dinner Eduard sat rigidly while the other couples relaxed and held each other. When I tried to touch him he pulled away.

'You see how they are together? That's how normal couples act,' I told Eduard quietly. He didn't respond.

The owner's three-year-old daughter was still up, and she played and threw herself on her parents. I thought about Paul's boys.

Eduard was drinking white wine and I kept refilling his glass. I thought he might relax and enjoy himself. It was a New Year's Eve party. We should try to have fun.

When I went to the bathroom I saw bottles of wine on a stand and I took one to the bathroom with me. I used a nail file to push the cork in and hid it in a cabinet under the sink. I checked my teeth to make sure they weren't purple from the red wine.

We were a hit at the party — I put on the best show I could, to prove to Eduard that I belonged. The junkie's boyfriend and I talked about Almodovar movies, impressing each other. In a slightly different life, I thought, it might just as well have been this one.

When we left Eduard was happy. He'd had a nice time. He was drunk and had his arm around me, and was laughing. We were imitating people at the party the way we liked to. They'd invited us to spend the night, but I whispered in his ear: 'Can you imagine waking up to these people?'

In the jeep, before we drove off, I turned to him and said, 'Her name is Brett. It's a silly name. It's a boy's name.'

27

We fought that night — we missed the fireworks — and all the next day, between having sex and me hurrying off 'to buy a Coke Light.' I was doing shots of tequila at a bar a couple of blocks from our place. Then we drove south, to the very southern end of the country, and had four tranquil nights in a guesthouse owned by some ex-pats in a town so small that no one knows it's there. It is hidden in a wildlife preserve and the other guests were marine biologists from California who swam a mile in the ocean every morning, and had come to snorkel and scuba dive on the reef.

We took a kayak out. We saw a sea turtle in the water and we tried to keep up with it in our kayak. Every time I thought it had disappeared he found it again hiding near one of the many little reefs and coral buds. We went a long way out, trying to reach a point that was miles from our hotel — I knew we'd be lucky if we made it halfway — and stopped on a deserted beach, and walked for a while, and looked in tide pools. I wanted to show him an octopus hiding. On one beach a woman came out and told us we had to move our kayak, and then we saw that it was a small hotel, and the beach was nude. The woman was loud and rude because she thought we had come to look at naked people. But there was no one but us anywhere you looked. We held hands as we walked and we kissed and I wondered if I should make love to him in some hidden spot — I had often made love to Paul in the sand, and it had always been awkward and fun — but I was tired and I didn't want to. When we were back in the water I asked Eduard if he could do the paddling for a while and I lay back and closed my eyes with a towel under my head. When I asked if he wanted help getting us back to the house he flexed his bicep for me and I laughed. The tide was against us and the sun was going down so after half an hour or so I started paddling again.

We made it back just as the sun set. He pulled the kayak up and lifted it into its wooden stand. I leaned the paddles against the side of the house. We had sex in the hammock.

'This has been the only place I really like in Nicaragua,' he said. 'I liked all our places,' I lied. 'But this was my favorite.'

28

Eduard had moved out of his condo and bought a house. He was having a housewarming party. I wasn't invited.

'I already bought my ticket. I'm going to be in town. If you want me to stay with you I will. Or if you want some space I'll stay in a hotel.'

'Of course you're staying with me,' Eduard said. 'I'm excited that you're coming. I'm just not ready to make a public announcement that we're a couple.'

'Everybody already knows, Eduard. All of your friends know more than I would have told them, if I lived there. You're the one who talks.'

'I'm not ready for you to meet Grace and Reynaldo.'

They were a famous couple in Panama, in their seventies, real money — Reynaldo's father had supplied the concrete when they built the canal. They were both recovered alcoholics. They had been friends of Eduard's for years and were like parents to Eduard. They had tried to make him stay at their place during the breakup with Lurisia. I had the impression that they thought well of me. When Eduard quoted them back to me they were usually speaking in my defense, or at least in defense of the possibility of our relationship. Unlike his other friends, who always seemed to me to insist that we were doomed.

'All of my friends think you're a falling down drunk.'

'Eduard, please. All of your friends are falling down drunks.'

He was quiet for a minute. Then he said, 'You're right. Fair enough. Except Grace and Reynaldo. It's true. They are all alcoholics. It's not like you'd be the only drunk there.'

'And Grace and Reynaldo understand. They quit drinking for a reason.'

'I know.'

He was good about that. If I disagreed with him, he'd listen, think it through, and if he were wrong, he'd revise his opinion. There aren't many people like that.

In fact most people are just the opposite. The more you disagree with them, the more committed they become to the lie they're telling you, or themselves, or the both of you.

There was something Eduard wasn't telling me. I asked him if Lurisia was coming to the party and he said, 'I doubt it. But it would be fine if she were. She'll bring her new boyfriend.' She had started dating a poet. I supposed they had met in her clinic.

29

I flew down. We christened the house. The day of the party Eduard was meeting a potential for lunch. He was a very successful developer and he was considering moving from his banker to Eduard. This was the man who would renovate all the hotels in Cuba, when it finally happened, and build the new ones. He had already signed a contract for the Peninsula Havana, and a Four Seasons Resort outside Santiago de Cuba.

'Just stay in bed,' he told me. 'I've got to hurry.'

I wouldn't let him out of bed until we'd had sex several times, and finally he stopped us and said, 'Really. I can't be late for this.'

'I'll come with you.'

'You can't come with me.'

'Not to the lunch, dummy. I'll ride in the cab and work while you're at your lunch. You can meet me after.'

We still hadn't figured out whether I could come to his party, or where I was going to spend the night if I wasn't invited. After a year of hiding things from each other and the people around us, it was a habit. We could leave something unspoken right until the moment of crisis.

When we got out of the cab I kissed him and wished him good luck.

We agreed to meet at a pizza place we both liked after his lunch.

He hurried away, walking that 'important businessman' walk of his that he walked sometimes and didn't suit him.

I found a restaurant to have a coffee. It was a nice place and they were empty except for me. The owner was opening wine bottles for his waitstaff to try, so they would know what to recommend, and he offered me a glass. I accepted, and he continued to offer me glasses from each new bottle. I warned him that my guest was arriving soon, and I didn't want him to know I had been drinking. He avoided me after that, and a waiter brought me a glass of water.

When Eduard came, I was drunk.

He told me the developer wanted to do business. He looked at me. I looked back at him and smiled. I didn't bother to try to hide the fact that I was drunk, or to lie about it. I shrugged.

'So I've been thinking, and I'd like a thirty-day break,' he said. He sat down. He paused. 'I mean, Brett, what am I supposed to say at this point?'

'It's over,' I said. 'We don't need a break.'

I wouldn't have had the courage to say what we both knew was true if I hadn't been drunk.

The waiter came. I ordered him a glass of champagne to celebrate his new client. They'd promote him to senior partner for this one. They'd give him a piece of the bank.

'You may as well have a glass, too,' he said.

I ordered a second glass. We toasted. He took a sip of his wine, and then put down his glass and said, 'I can't do this, Brett.' He walked out. I looked at the champagne and realized I didn't want it either. But I sat there and drank the two glasses and paid the check.

30

Miguel's on Hermosa opens at 11 a.m. and was walking distance from the library. It was under new management so they didn't know me from the old days and wouldn't chase me away. The bartender poured me real drinks. I had five vodka sodas and I don't remember leaving the bar. I had to meet a real estate agent about a house I wanted to rent. During the walk I realized how drunk I was and I called Sadie.

'Tell me honestly,' I said. 'You can hear I'm having a bit of trouble.' She made that kind noise she makes.

'I have a meeting. About a house. It's important. I have to have a house. I promised Paul. Do you think I can go?'

'I think maybe you should skip it this time. Are you going to be okay? Do you want me to call you a ride home?'

'No, I'm okay. I'm supposed to already have the house today. I'm supposed to take his boys tonight.'

'Maybe you could take a nap? Brett, I think you should text Paul to change the day, then go back to the hotel and lie down for a bit.'

'Sadie. Usually if someone's in a bad situation, they don't want the truth.'

I went to the bar at The Raphael. I had to pick up the boys at Paul's at five. I found out later that they bounced me from The Raphael bar that afternoon.

When I checked back into the hotel a few weeks later my favorite bartender told me, after I apologized: 'That's fine. But I can't serve you down here anymore. It's from the management. You'll have to use your minibar.' He was stern and I wondered if I'd taken off my clothes or invited him up to my room. I have lost bartenders that way before.

31

I remember parts of the drive to get the boys. The auto parts store on El Novio and Hermosa. Telling myself not to take a left there. The red light and the cop who waved at me while everyone honked. An Outkast song on the radio. I was elated and turned it up. Headed the wrong way on a one-way side street near Paul's house and trying to do a three-point turn, then giving up and taking the straightest way.

I don't remember arriving at the house, or how I convinced Bella to leave, or what game or movie I started playing for them. Thinking back on it now, I expect they were hungry for dinner. Or maybe Bella had made something.

Bella called Paul, and I do remember when he got to the house. I think I asked him not to shout in front of the boys. I can remember him putting me in his car. He told me I had been lying down in the kitchen with macaroni and cheese boiling over on the stove.

'I want to spend the night here!' I screamed, and Paul said, 'Brett, you are not well right now.' His ten-year-old stood silently, immobile, in the front door of the house. He was following his father's requests carefully and quickly. The sunlight was bright and Paul wouldn't listen to anything I said. 'I'm okay,' I told him. 'Please let me stay. Yes I had a couple of drinks. But let me stay. Paul, please let me stay. I just want to stay.'

32

After Paul dropped me at The Raphael I ran a hot bath. I called room service and asked for a shaving razor and a bottle of scotch. I took all my valium, broke the bit of razor out of the plastic, and called Eduard. The veins were slippery little devils and with the sliver of razor I was only able to get the ones on my left wrist. It's harder than it looks. I cut the thumb and fingers of my right hand doing it.

When we got off the phone Eduard called Paul, and soon, as the water was turning pink and all the light in the room seemed to go pink along with it, Paul and the manager came in the bathroom, and they lifted me up out of the tub like I was a bubble and carried me to the hospital.

33

When Eduard was still living with Lurisia, we were walking in Panama City, in the shade in a park, under the purple trees, holding hands, and he said: 'I enjoy living a double life. I don't want to face the truth.' He was being playful but he meant it. I said, 'That's almost exactly what Anna Karenina says.'

The illusions we depended on about love and each other were necessary to keep us going. Yes, it all collapsed. But afterwards, I think we both wondered, will I ever have something that good again?

Acknowledgments

My deepest thanks to the gracious and patient monks and other Buddhist friends at the Kungri Monastery in the Pin Valley, India, where this manuscript was first written; to Wayne and the gang at UMKC; to Tim Small, the kind editor who first conceived of, motivated and published the project overseas; to Lorin Stein and my all-knowing, all-good agent Susan Golomb, who together convinced me to rewrite what began as a memoir into fiction; to my brilliant editor Giancarlo DiTrapano, who has been relentless in his determination to see it appear here in the US, and who has quite possibly put as much passion into the book as I have; to Mom, Alicia, Rebecca, Darren, Pat and Mompat; to Rinpoche; and above all, to my daughters, Zelly, Margaret and Portia, and to my best reader, best friend, and loving wife, Amie.

We do hope that you have enjoyed reading this large print book.

Did you know that all of our titles are available for purchase?

We publish a wide range of high quality large print books including:
Romances, Mysteries, Classics
General Fiction
Non Fiction and Westerns

Special interest titles available in large print are:
The Little Oxford Dictionary
Music Book
Song Book
Hymn Book
Service Book

Also available from us courtesy of Oxford University Press:
Young Readers' Dictionary
(large print edition)
Young Readers' Thesaurus
(large print edition)

For further information or a free brochure, please contact us at:
Ulverscroft Large Print Books Ltd.,
The Green, Bradgate Road, Anstey,
Leicester, LE7 7FU, England.
Tel: (00 44) 0116 236 4325
Fax: (00 44) 0116 234 0205

Other titles published by Ulverscroft:

MUNICH AIRPORT

Greg Baxter

An American expat in London receives a piece of news that is nearly incomprehensible: the body of his sister Miriam has been found in her Berlin apartment, dead from starvation. Three weeks later, the man, his elderly father, and an American consular official find themselves in the fogbound Munich Airport, where Miriam's coffin is to be loaded onto a commercial jet. Slowly, the trio's stories of those weeks unfold: time spent waiting for Miriam's body to be released, sifting through her possessions, puzzling over the mystery of her awful death — and trying to comprehend and share in her suffering, her yearning, and her grace.

THE PONZI MAN

Declan Lynch

John Devlin has lost all that he owned —
plus all that a lot of other people owned
— through internet gambling. His once-
celebrated financial genius has made him
notorious, and now they call him the
Ponzi Man. Awaiting trial for the theft of
his clients' money, John goes to live in an
old caravan at the seaside resort where he
used to work as a teenager. But while his
solicitor James attempts to persuade him
to embark upon a rehabilitation pro-
gramme and so reduce his sentence, John
is instead contemplating one last big
play . . .

A MEAL IN WINTER

Hubert Mingarelli

One morning in the dead of winter, three German soldiers are dispatched into the frozen Polish countryside to track down any Jews they can find — and return them for execution. Having captured a young man hiding in the woods, they rest in an abandoned house before continuing back to camp. But before long, the group's sympathies have splintered as they consider the moral implications of their mission, and confront their own consciences. Should the Jew be offered food? And after breaking bread with a man, how can they possibly send him to his death — or risk everything to return him to liberty?